FIRST FLURRIES

ALSO BY JOANNE DEMAIO

first flurries

A NOVEL

JOANNE DEMAIO

Copyright © 2018 Joanne DeMaio
All rights reserved.

ISBN: 1723467987
ISBN-13: 978-1723467981

www.joannedemaio.com

To the cottage owners
who set their Santa decoration at the curb

I picked him up and wrote this story.

one

IT'S TIME TO LEAVE.

Lindsey passes red barns and white picket fences along the winding country road. When she drives by a man raking the last of autumn's brown leaves, or a young couple walking a dog, they all stop and wave at her. She gives her horn a friendly tap, accustomed to the attention now. Something about seeing the tiny house towed behind her SUV brings out that happy response in passersby. Might as well call her tiny house a happy house. It makes people smile.

A favorite part of this autumn road trip has been seeing the old New England towns via the back roads. Even now, she drives past saltbox colonials and Victorian farmhouses with withering cornstalks tied to lampposts; with swirls of dry leaves blowing across frosty lawns. Soon, front porches will be strung with twinkling lights; wreaths hung on doors.

Still, there's always a tinge of sadness when she hitches

1

up her house and hits the road again. Especially after meeting so many nice folks this fall, no matter where she parked her pop-up clothing boutique: a flea market in Maine, street festivals in New Hampshire.

But after spending a few months towing her shop-on-wheels to craft fairs all across New England, she has to move on. This time, though, Lindsey's not sure where her next stop will be. A few empty weeks loom in front of her. They're holiday weeks, too. It would be nice to find a cozy place to unhitch her house for a bit, maybe find a Christmastime bazaar or winter expo that might also welcome her little shop among its vendors.

With the highway entrance only blocks ahead, she gives a lingering last look at this pretty street. But wait! Lindsey leans forward, squinting through the windshield. What's that? Though her destination is unknown, one thing's for certain, anyway. After spending the past year on the road, she's become expert at slamming on the brakes for vintage treasures relegated roadside.

Today, she does it again.

While carefully pulling over her SUV and its hitched tiny house, her eyes are already inspecting the large Santa decoration propped on the grass, curbside. It's an old-world Santa Claus—he's thin, and wears a long, burgundy velvet robe that reaches to the top of his black lace-up boots. With his mittened hand, he holds over his shoulder a canvas sack looped with thick twine and tarnished jingle bells. Greens and berries nestled around a wrapped present peek out from the sack. By the looks of him, this Santa must be about three feet tall. He stands on a painted wooden base beside a spindly, artificial fir tree strung with red berries and miniature gift boxes. The tree is topped with a gold felt star.

But most importantly, a cardboard sign is looped over that treetop. A sign reading: *Santa Needs A New Home! FREE.*

It's enough to get Lindsey to turn off her SUV and jump out. She fusses a little with Santa's wide black belt, and with the wavy white beard reaching down his chest. What she likes about this Santa is that he's *so* old-fashioned looking, like the regal Saint Nicks appearing on antique Christmas cards. Which makes him perfectly suited to her mobile shop, *Vagabond Vintage*—if only he could fit somewhere in the tiny space. Regardless, he's too good to pass up. In three seconds flat, Lindsey scoops up this classic Santa and stands him in the passenger seat of her SUV.

"Perfect," she whispers, giving him a pat before rushing around and getting in the driver's side once more. Turning the key in the ignition, she glances over at Santa riding shotgun beside her.

Then? Well, then Lindsey puts her SUV in gear and drives off toward the highway. With a nod of her head, she declares, "Santa needs a new home, and golly gumdrops ... so do I!"

～○

With the long box hoisted up on his shoulder, Greg Davis maneuvers his father's narrow basement stairs. It's a

Victorian house, after all. And the stairs are steep, too, so they give him a workout he hadn't counted on today. He'd planned on going for a jog to get ready for the upcoming Santa's Run 5K, but now he won't have to with all this huffing and puffing.

"These old houses," he mutters beneath his breath.

His father, Pete, stands in the kitchen. He's sipping a hot coffee while watching Greg from the cellar doorway. "You say something, son?"

Greg finagles himself through that doorway— bumping a kitchen wall with the Christmas tree box. He backs up a step and realigns things before turning to the hallway, then into the living room. Sunlight shines through the lace panel curtains there.

"Where do you want the tree, Dad?" Greg stops in the middle of the room. "Same place as always?"

"You bet. In the corner near the fireplace. You can open the box right there."

So as Greg lifts out faux branches on the threadbare Oriental rug, the familiar tree gets built once more. Limb by limb, it takes shape the same way it has for years now.

"I was just going to help you set it up, Dad, before going for a run," Greg admits as he straightens the pre-lit branches, cramped from being stuffed in the box. "But I guess I can hang some ornaments with you, too."

"That'd be nice. I remember the year your mother picked out this tree," Pete answers, his voice wistful. "Got it at the old five-and-dime."

"Yeah, well. Better wash your hands afterward. I've

heard there's lead in some of these artificial trees."

Pete opens a plastic tote and lifts out a box of bell ornaments. "That's my boy," he's saying as he does. "The good doctor always looking out for me."

"Yup. Good and responsible," Greg gripes under his breath again while fussing with lights on a branch.

Just then, Pete gives Greg a red glitter bell to hang. "Your mother looked forward to hanging her bell collection every year. Would give each bell a little jingle." Pete rings one now, and the melodic *ting-a-ling* fills the room. "What a happy time that was. Someday? You'll have that, too."

"Eh." From the other side of the tree, Greg glances at his father. He's got on a thin cardigan over a flannel shirt, and flecks of wood shavings dot the cuffs. "Maybe."

Next, Pete lifts out two wooden deer from the tote. The deer—a doe and a buck—are spray-painted a pale gold, and the buck's antlers swirl over its head.

"Those the deer you gave Mom?" Greg asks.

"First pair I ever whittled. Love deer," Pete answers as he sets them on the mantel. He turns to Greg. "How about you? You seeing anybody, son?"

"No. And I'll tell you something, Dad. I'm done trying this year." Greg loops a needle-pointed Santa onto a tree branch. "Seriously."

"Don't say that. You're a handsome fella. Clean cut, in good shape. A nice guy."

"Right. And maybe that's the problem," Greg tells him as he steps back and considers the tree. "I shave every morning, iron my lab coat. Bring pastries in for the staff.

For what, Dad? Because you know that saying, nice guys finish last? I'm living proof."

"That's nonsense."

"Really?" Greg lifts two black lanterns from another box and sets them on the hearth. "Then explain this. The past three Christmases have brought me nothing but holiday heartbreak. I struck out with three beautiful women each year. And look at Wes."

"Wes? What's your brother have to do with it?"

"I'm just saying. Two years ago, his fiancée broke off their engagement, and so Wes was suddenly single. For about a *week* before he was spoken for again. Met Jane right on his mail route, for crying out loud! And now he *is* married, easy as pie. Yet I can't seem to ever get the girl. So … what's the matter with me?"

"Nothing, you hear?" Pete insists as he sets faux green garland around the love deer on his fireplace mantel. "Nothing at all. You've worked hard to get a commendable career established as an orthopedic surgeon. And you assisted with your mother when she was ill. All that hasn't left a whole lot of time to find the right doe."

When Greg—hanging patchwork stockings from the mantel—glares at his father, Pete shrugs before turning on the Christmas tree's twinkling lights. "You just stay busy living your life," his father tells him while setting one of the tree's glitter bells a-jingling. "Paths cross when you least expect it."

○

The next day, Lindsey continues making her uncertain way along the interstate. She eventually leaves Massachusetts behind and enters Connecticut. The day is all blue skies and crisp, cold air. It strikes her how the landscape noticeably changes from one state to another. Here, the view is of farmland, cow pastures, wooded areas and rural towns dotted with white-steepled chapels.

Passing different Connecticut town signs, she cruises along with her newly found old-world Santa Claus propped on the passenger seat. Every now and then someone gives a happy horn beep at the sight of the shingled house towed behind her SUV. Since last January, Lindsey's whole life has been towed behind her, actually: her tiny vintage shop, in her tiny house, all comprising her tiny life. And all of it—the bucolic sights, the friendly folks, the freedom to chart her own course—has her humming lightly to a song on the radio.

When a local meteorologist comes on and gives the weather report forecasting a clear, breezy December day, Lindsey's glad to hear it. Because the nice thing about her life is that it's tiny enough to simply see where the winter wind will blow her next. It's a thought that has her consider an upcoming sign for the town of Wethersfield. But she's not moved to take that exit and land there, so she keeps on driving.

The thing is, if the winter winds don't decide for her, Lindsey can always turn to her magical snow globe. When she's on the road like this, it sits in the cup holder beside her. One good shake and it looks like the wind's a-blowin' right *inside* that glass globe—stirring up hundreds of tiny swirling snowflakes around a lone, wise snowman. Knowing she's always been a dreamer, Lindsey's father gave her the snow globe as a gift last year when she downsized and bought her tiny house. But it's when she recites the special verse penned in his gift card that a certain magic seems cast upon her, guiding her way.

Passing another highway exit and still hesitant about where to stop and unhitch, Lindsey reaches for that snow globe. She flips it so the snowflakes spin and twirl, then sets it back down, all while reciting the lines memorized from her father's card.

"Unsure where to go? Give a little shake … and your heart will always know."

After glancing down at that lone snowman standing watch beneath the globe's now-falling flakes, she reads the next approaching highway sign. ENTERING ADDISON.

With the sign scarcely behind her, she gives it a double take. "Addison, Addison," she quietly says, trying to place its familiarity. Beyond the highway, smoke curls from cozy homes; a ribbon of silver river glints in the sunlight; a flock of geese flies toward a barren cornfield. Catching sight of a log cabin then, it comes to her.

"Uncle Gus!" she exclaims, thinking of her father's brother … and of the little lakeside cabin community where he lives. She pats the snow globe beside her, whispering, "It worked!"

And for the next half mile driving toward the exit ramp, she softly sings, *"O little town of Addison,"* until she hits the blinker and veers off the highway, into the heart of a charming town seeming straight out of a snow globe itself.

two

LATER THAT DAY, LINDSEY IS in wanderlust heaven. Because this is one of her favorite things about being footloose and following the winter wind: exploring picturesque New England towns. But being so taken by this town of Addison—with its historic homes and darling little country boutiques—she's so busy looking at the grand doorways and shop windows, the surprise comes upon her unexpectedly.

"Oh no!" She leans forward and squints out the windshield. A block ahead, with no easy turnoff beforehand, is a traffic roundabout. A roundabout in the direct path of her and her hitched tiny house. "Hmm," she says, carefully slowing down her SUV. "Okay, you've got this," she assures herself.

After yielding at the roundabout entrance, she maneuvers her vehicle smoothly into the circular traffic flow: moving cautiously, gauging distance to the curb, keeping an eye on incoming vehicles, and trying like *heck* to read the abundance of traffic signs mounted roadside. This particular roundabout seems unusually narrow, congested and distracting—its signs stating *Merge*; *No Stops*; *Pedestrian Crossing*; *Trucks–No Turns*; *Slow*. It takes all her attention to simply get around the circling roadway—which she does, thank you very much.

Problem is, she finds herself right where she began—still in that roundabout! So she continues with another go-around, all the while reaching for her snow globe and giving it a quick, hopeful shake.

"*Unsure where to go?*" she whispers. "*Give a little shake ... and your heart will always know.*"

When she comes upon the next turnoff veering right, away she goes. With nary a glance back at the quirky, too-small roundabout in her rearview mirror, Lindsey continues on her merry way along the streets of this quaint New England village.

Merrily lost now, too.

She passes a town green and a café called Whole Latte Life. But the lakeside community where her uncle lives wouldn't be on a commercial, busy road. On a whim, she turns off at the next street, then after a few blocks, takes a left onto Old Willow Road. Here, farmhouses, Cape Cods and English Tudors line the wide street. The country homes sit on large yards edged with white picket fences, or low stone walls. There are lantern-lit porticos and open front porches gracing many of the houses' entranceways.

When she spots an older woman walking a dog on the

next block, Lindsey carefully pulls over and rolls down the window. "Excuse me!" she calls out while leaning past the old-world Santa in the passenger seat. "I'm a little bit lost. Can you tell me how to get to … Snowflake Lake?"

"Oh!" Holding her dog's leash close, the woman steps to the curb. "Is that one of those tiny houses?" She motions to Lindsey's shingled house hitched behind her SUV.

"Yes, it is!" Lindsey still leans past Santa.

"Do you *live* in that?" The woman steps back, unable to take her eyes off of Lindsey's petite house-on-a-trailer.

"Why, I do, actually."

"How do you like that, Pepper?" The woman pats her small black dog. "A genuine tiny house, just like a gingerbread cottage." She looks back to Lindsey then, while stepping to the SUV and peering in the passenger window past Santa, who she also gives a gentle pat. "And where *do* you live, in your cute little home?"

"Well, that's the thing. I travel all over. But if you could just point me to Snowflake Lake?"

"Snowflake Lake. Oh, it's such a secluded spot here in Addison. You go … thataway." The nosy woman points farther down the street. "All the way to the end of Old Willow Road. It's hard to see, but a dirt road veers off into the woods there. It's only one lane. And," she says while leaning back and eyeing Lindsey's tiny house, "it's *very* narrow."

"Don't worry, I can manage!" Lindsey puts her SUV in gear. "Thank you so much," she says, giving the horn a toot as she drives off.

Passing more farmhouses and country homes, Lindsey rounds a curve in the road, soon finding out that the woman wasn't kidding about the turn-off lane being narrow. More surprising, though, as Lindsey turns onto that lane, are the frost heaves. Driving over them, her hitched house lurches this way and that! She takes a deep breath and tries steering *around* the heaves. But upon another good jostle, she has to grab up her snowman snow globe and hold it close so it doesn't fall and break.

Finally, she enters a small parking lot, gets out and walks toward the distant lakeside cabins. "Blue Jay Bungalow," she murmurs, remembering her uncle's place. When she passes one cabin, she sees a deer on the other side of a crystal-clear lake. If you'd call it that. It's small, and more of a pond—one as peaceful as can be.

Suddenly, a fondness comes back to her from when she visited here with her parents when she was in high school. It has her smile, because yes, this is one of those special places where nothing ever changes. Here, memories from years ago seem to still be happening—if you glance *just* right at the shadowy pines, or at the benches set lakeside—as if time stands perfectly still.

On any other day, Lindsey might take a leisurely stroll around the lake. Might pause and smile at all the bird-themed cabin names: Robin Residence, Sparrow Suite, Hawk Hut, Finch Farmhouse.

But not today.

When she spots Blue Jay Bungalow, it feels like coming home again. So she hurries up the porch steps and wastes no time giving the carved woodpecker doorknocker a chipper *rat-a-tat-tat-tat*!

⌒∾⌒

The management at Joel's Bar and Grille didn't waste any time. As soon as Thanksgiving was over, out came the Christmas décor. Greg looks over at the red neon bells flashing and blinking in the bar's front window. Blinking and flashing, again and again.

On. Off. On ... Off.

Which is all Greg needs to see, those jolly red bells reminding him of his still-single status this holiday season. For the past three years, the possibility of romance has been the same for him—on, then off. On ... Off. Raising his hopes, then dashing them. So this year, he's keeping the love switch set to *Off.*

Getting back to the dartboard in front of him, he raises a dart and throws it. *Zing!* Then he takes a swig of his soda before stepping aside for his brother's turn.

"Lame," Greg says—kind of to himself, kind of not. "Everything's lame. Saturday night and I'm having a *soda* with my brother? What am I? Twelve?"

"No," Wes answers with a glance over his shoulder. "You're thirty-five, smart and responsible. You know," he says as he cuffs his flannel shirtsleeves, then flicks his first dart. "Drinking only soda while you're on call with the hospital. Concerned about your job."

"And stuck in a rut."

"What are you talking about?"

"A woman rut." Greg grabs a handful of pretzels from a basket on their nearby table. "Here it is, the first day of December," he says while tossing a few of those salty pretzels in his mouth, "and I'm alone again for another Christmas season. I'm not even going to try this year. Not going through this anymore. This holiday heartbreak."

Wes throws another dart—*thwack!* "You're just tired, Scrubs. Worked some long shifts this week. You'll feel better in the morning."

"Wrong, Wes. The past three Christmases, I struck out. Swing and a miss, times three." When Greg takes another soda swig, he glances around the dark room, past the swags of silver garland strung from the ceiling. Lots of holiday cheer is going down tonight. Beer toasts around the bar—where two giant nutcrackers stand sentry at either end. Songs jingling on the jukebox. And couples kissing under the mistletoe. "I'm telling you, I'm not going through another disappointing holiday season," Greg continues. "This time around, if I don't even try, there won't be any pain."

Just then, two women walk past them at the dartboard. After one gives a small wave, Wes nudges him. "What about her?" Wes asks.

Greg looks over at the brunette. "What, because she said hi? That's your pickup line? *Hi?*"

Wes watches the two women heading to a distant table. "You're probably better off alone, anyway. I live in a house *full* of women. Jane, and my mother-in-law—okay, she lives in the carriage house, but she's constantly popping in. And Jane's sister, Chloe, is *always* stopping by with her two girls. Heck, I'm the lone stag in that old farmhouse."

Whump! Wes throws his third dart.

"At least you *have* a wife." Greg picks up his three darts. "But for me, the topic of women is off the table this year. I've had enough. During the past three Christmases, I've dated three lovely ladies and had three strikeouts. And each one broke my heart." He assumes his throwing position while spinning a dart in his fingers.

"Come on, it hasn't been *that* bad." Wes lifts his beer and takes a long swallow. Behind him, over at the bar, hoots and hollers rise as another happy couple locks lips in a long holiday kiss beneath the mistletoe.

"Hasn't been that bad?" Greg repeats while glancing at the romantic couple before turning back to the game at hand. He raises his dart so it's level with his line of vision. "Easy for you to say, bro," Greg argues, holding the dart steady. "But me? I'm done. First there was …" He pauses then, while releasing his dart and watching it thwack into the dartboard. "First there was Vera. Thought for sure she was the girl for me a few years ago. Had a nice dance and a few laughs at her sister's wedding, but nope. Derek Cooper cut in." Greg levels a second dart at the board. "Now that one? That one's for Jane. I know she was meant for you," he says while nodding at Wes. "But still. I had a do-si-do with that delicate doe, and my hay-bale dance led to no romance." He clasps his brother's shoulder. "I'm happy for you, though. Sort of."

Wes raises his beer glass in a pseudo toast. "To my bride, Jane," he says. "It's almost been a year now, since our wedding. Can you believe it?"

"A year." Greg picks up his third dart. "And a year ago, it was Penny for me. Pretty Penny Hart, who pierced my hopeful heart there at Snowflake Lake." Greg shifts his stance and raises the dart. "I had high hopes for that copper-haired beauty. Tried to watch a Christmas movie with a crooning Bing in her cozy cabin. But you just *know* it'll be Frank Lombardo who'll put on the diamond ring. And I'll be left with another dateless night at yet another town wedding. So, Penny?" Greg raises his dart and takes aim. "This one's for you," he says as he zings the dart through the air to the distant dartboard. *Thwack!*

Shrugging it all off—the darts game, women—Greg follows Wes to their nearby table, where their buffalo chicken wraps await. "Three strikes and I'm *out*. Out of the game of love," he tells his brother as he clinks his soda glass to Wes' beer. "This season? I'm sidelined, sitting romance out on the bench."

❧

Maybe what Lindsey loves about her uncle Gus' cabin is that it's small, so she *truly* feels right at home. And that it's cozy … with its wood-planked floors and walls, and its silver-blue painted trim around the paned windows overlooking the serene lake.

Or maybe it's simply the nostalgia she feels sitting at Gus' dining room table that evening and sipping from a cup of steaming hot cocoa doused with miniature marshmallows—just like she did as a child visiting here long ago.

Sweet nostalgia is one of the best feelings to have. It's why she sells *vintage* clothes. The same nostalgic feeling comes with her boutique's inventory.

"My brother didn't mention that you'd be in town, Lindsey," her uncle Gus tells her now. He sits at the table with his own cocoa, his eyes twinkling with happiness beneath bushy white eyebrows.

Lindsey shrugs. "Dad didn't really know. And neither did I! I like to sometimes go wherever the wind takes me."

"But how do you get by? I mean, you need to earn a living."

"I *do* earn a living! With my very own business, Uncle Gus. It's right inside my tiny house." She stands up and extends a hand to him. "Come on, I'll show you."

So after putting on coats and hats, they take their cocoa cups outside. As the sun goes down, they walk along the leaf-strewn, wooded path leading to the little parking lot where she left her house, still hitched to her SUV.

"I have a pop-up shop," she explains while nodding toward her tiny one-level house with a small, peaked loft. The house's cedar shingles are golden, its wide window and door trim painted bright white. "Vagabond Vintage.

I sell the vintage clothing that I've *always* been into, and some home accessories, too. What's nice," she says to Gus, who is utterly taken with the tiny, portable house, "is that I can set up shop anywhere I go. And I have an online store, too."

"My goodness," Gus remarks as he walks up the few steps to her door. "It looks just like a mini cabin!" He looks at her from beneath the brim of his tweed cap. "But how do customers find you if you're not established somewhere?"

"Social media," Lindsey says as she unlocks the door. "I actually have a pretty good online following that spreads the word." She motions Gus inside, explaining, "I announce whenever I'm setting up in a new town, post photos of my latest vintage finds, and my local followers either stop by or send their friends."

Gus walks down the short hallway, where a rack of clothes is organized by decade and strapped into place on a side wall. "Well, I'll be … Where do you get all this stuff?"

"That depends, Uncle Gus. Estate sales, big flea markets, and even bidding online for special pieces. Sometimes curb-alerts, too. Folks put out free things at the curb. I shine them up and they make it to a shop shelf," she says.

"Is that right?" Gus asks. "You know, I still have some of Betty's things from before she passed on. Maybe you'd like something for your shop?"

"Oh, Aunt Betty had such a flair for style. That would

be wonderful." Lindsey sets her cocoa mug on a small table and turns to Gus. "Come on, I'll give you the grand tour."

It doesn't take long. In a few minutes, Lindsey shows how she displays the vintage clothing in a doorless closet when her shop's open; sets up a register on the kitchen countertop; and explains how the bathroom—with its foldaway toilet—doubles as a tiny dressing room. "With the right shelving and counter space, customers don't even realize it's a bathroom. As a matter of fact, *everything* is portable and easily moved, *and* secured." She points up to a loft. "My bedroom is up there, an area off-limits to customers."

"But how do you fit all your things in here?" Gus asks, looking up toward the small loft.

Lindsey demonstrates how her sofa is made of three upholstered lift-top boxes pressed together. "Storage is key," she adds, pointing out built-in drawers under the loft stairs.

"And what's this?" Gus asks when he sits at her tiny dining table while nodding to a large framed map on the wall there.

"I glued the map to corkboard before I framed it," Lindsey explains. "So I can do this." She plucks a red pushpin out of a cup, then pulls a green pin out of the map in the Massachusetts square. "*Green* pushpins signify either where I'm going, or where I'm currently staying."

"And the red pins?"

"When I pack up and leave a town, I change the pin

to *red*, to note all the places I've stopped at and visited." She steps back and nods to the trail of red pins snaking from Maine to Connecticut—showing her recent autumn route. "So this one," she says as she raises the red pin, then pushes it in among the many pushpins already dotting the United States map, "marks my stay in Northampton."

"You've covered a lot of the East Coast, I see," Gus says, standing for a better look at the pinned map.

"I followed a craft fair route all fall. Started at a big flea market in Maine—and ended up right at Snowflake Lake." Lindsey picks a green pushpin out of her pin cup. "Here. I'd like you to have the honors, Uncle Gus."

"Honors? Of what?"

"Of marking Addison on my map, now that I've arrived."

Gus takes the green pin, and as he's pushing it into the state of Connecticut, tells Lindsey about a new holiday festival in town.

"It's called Merry Market. Local business owners set up shop on the town green. It's a really popular stop on my Holly Trolley tours. Maybe you can bring Vagabond Vintage there. Folks would love shopping right inside this tiny house!"

"That sounds promising, Uncle Gus. But it's so last minute, do you think there would be space for me and my little shop?"

"I'll pull a few strings," he says, patting her hand. "Make a phone call or two. But first, you need a place to live. And I have the perfect spot in mind for your tiny house."

"Really?"

Gus nods. "Right here! There's a very small camping area on the western side of the lake—a hop, skip and a jump from my place. Room enough for three RVs when folks like to camp in the summer months. Do a little fishing, hiking. But the camp spots are vacant now, and better yet, they come complete with electrical hookup and water supply. So you'll stay on at Snowflake Lake and be all set for a while."

"You'd do that for me, Uncle Gus?"

They turn to leave then. As Gus steps out and admires Lindsey's home-on-wheels, he assures her, "Glad to. You're family, Lindsey. Now. About that spot for your tiny house ... It's just the right size, between two tall pines. At the edge of the lake, too." He motions for her to follow him as he sips from his cocoa. "I'll show you where so you can settle right in."

Minutes later, the two of them arrive at a petite patch of cleared land in the woods, surrounded by tall pine trees filled with chirping cardinals and swooping black-capped chickadees, quieting now at day's end.

When Lindsey sees the vacant camp area, she knows.

Yes, she knows that her magical snow globe *never* steers her wrong. Because one shake of it on the highway this morning led her here, to Addison's enchanted woodland hideaway.

three

GREG COULDN'T BRING HIMSELF TO do it: to skip shaving.

Not that he didn't deliberate it, all on account of something his father had said. *You're a nice guy, son. Clean cut, responsible.*

Okay. But like Greg told his father, if he's a nice guy, then he's also living proof of something. There's no denying it, either. Not as another holiday season rolls in and he's still single and dateless.

Yes, he's living proof that *nice* guys finish last.

So an idea occurred to him to change.

Not to change being nice. But to change, well … *something*. His looks, for instance—which he could tweak by not shaving; instead sporting a shadow of whiskers, maybe. A change in appearance would at least be a *start* during this season when he's sitting things out on the bench.

A start to some sort of metamorphosis.

But first thing Monday morning, it becomes painfully obvious that old habits die hard when he goes straight from the shower to the bathroom sink, where he drags a razor down his face. Thoroughly, too, not missing a single spot—not one whisker.

It's not surprising. After all, he is a man of few changes. Even his choice of home—a condominium in a restored historic house—left old design details unchanged. From original 1759 millwork to wide-plank wood floors to antique light fixtures, much effort went into not changing the building's historic character.

"Maybe I have to do this change thing little by little," he admits to his reflection as he pats his face with a towel. "Become some *new* Greg Davis one step at a time." He rehangs the hand towel, a little crooked—so there! That's a change. "*And* … I'm not ironing my lab coat, *either*," he tells his reflection before flicking off the bathroom light.

When he's getting ready for work in the kitchen, as usual, the countertop TV is tuned to the local station. While the news anchors recap the day's headlines, Greg packs a lunch—same old ham sandwich—on the dark granite countertop. When he gets some paperwork together and is about to pour his coffee, meteorologist Leo Sterling cuts in with breaking news.

"Listen up, folks. First flurries will be hitting Addison this very morning! Yes, it's true. No matter you're cryin'—there'll be snowflakes a-flyin'!"

Greg shakes his head and shuts off the TV. "Swell," he mumbles as he heads to the coat closet and switches his good leather shoes to slushers. On his way out, he shuts off the coffeemaker in the kitchen. If it's time to change things up, might as well let someone else make the coffee. "I'll just sit at the window in Whole Latte Life and ... well, I'll watch those first flurries fall," he says to himself. But that's not all he does. He also gives a salute to the quiet TV, where moments ago Leo Sterling could barely contain his snow-excitement.

With that, Greg grabs his wrinkled lab coat, black leather bag, long wool coat and leather gloves, too, and heads out the door.

⌒≫○

Addison's streets are already feeling familiar. Lindsey hitched her tiny house to her SUV and drives down Old Willow Road now. She's heading to The Green, where Uncle Gus' town-hall connection wants to see her shop with his own two eyes. Said he cannot issue a permit without ensuring the business structure fits on the grounds.

So while listening to a local meteorologist give the forecast, Lindsey heads toward the town center. Up ahead, she spots The Green. It's several blocks long, surrounded by stately colonial homes and rambling farmhouses lining one side, and more houses, as well as a coffee shop and some boutiques lining the other. A few local businesses' tents and trailers are already set up in the designated Merry Market area.

While searching for a place to park her tiny house, a sudden squall of snowflakes drops from the sky. It's the type of gentle flurry that's nothing but delightful. As Lindsey circles The Green, those crystal flakes blow this way and that, distracting her enough so that she drives just past the parking entrance before realizing her mistake.

"Oh, bloomin' heck," she says while pulling over to the curb. If she can navigate backing up and making a partial K-turn, she can drive her tiny house, *and* tiny shop, straight into the Merry Market area and get that necessary legal permit to conduct business there.

"When the first flurries are falling to the ground," Leo Sterling is declaring on her radio as she shifts into reverse and slowly backs up, "stop a moment to take a look around!"

The snow squall keeps swirling as Lindsey concentrates on making a K-turn—back, then forward, then back again—to maneuver her tiny house onto The Green.

"First flurries are a magical sight," the meteorologist continues, "to always start your day off right!"

Hearing his words, Lindsey wants only that—to start this day off right. So she glances up through her windshield and suddenly feels like she's in her very own snow globe again. One that's just been tipped as the flakes swirl from the sky.

It's just what she needs: a little … yes, a little magic sprinkled on her new venture here in Addison. Once more, she steals another glimpse skyward while backing up her SUV. The white snowflakes … they're pretty and sparkling.

Tumbling and twirling … and … and … *Crunch!*

Instantly, Lindsey slams on the brakes, then grabs her own jostled snow globe to prevent its falling from the cup holder to the floor. With the vehicle stopped and her cherished snow globe safe, she leans back with a sigh.

A reluctant sigh—because it's back to reality now.

A painful reality as she sets down the snow globe and gets out of her SUV to assess whatever damage she just backed into.

꧁

One thing Greg did right today was to wear his slushers. Because that first flurry is actually accumulating and making for slushy sidewalks. Sitting at a café window table in Whole Latte Life, he sips from a coffee while waiting for his breakfast. Outside the frosty window, snow keeps falling and, well, it's starting to look a little like Christmas out there. Balsam garland wraps up coach-light lampposts on the town green, and in the distance, the red covered bridge is outlined in glimmering white lights.

Behind him, suddenly the quiet coffee shop is abuzz with chatter. *How charming!* and *Look how pretty!* Greg supposes it's because of the first snowfall, until he looks down the block a ways. On the other side of The Green, a shingled tiny house is being towed behind a large SUV. The house is petite enough to fit on a small trailer. Watching it move along, he can see that the cottage-like house is one level, with a peaked loft. The house is also sided with golden cedar shake shingles and has white-paned windows … rustic details giving it an almost fairy-tale look. The tiny house makes its way around the perimeter of The Green, all while more *oohs* and *aahs* fill the cozy café.

"Think a tall guy like yourself could fit in one of those?" Greg's waitress asks as she sets down his food and pats his shoulder.

"How about that …" he remarks while watching the trailered house. "It's something to see."

After refilling his coffee cup, the waitress tells him as she breezes off, "Well, you're all set to jump-start your day now."

Greg shifts his attention to his grilled-and-buttered muffin bursting with blueberries. He bites into the pastry, then sips from his steaming coffee while watching that tiny house circle The Green before it stops near Whole Latte Life. So he gets a good look at it up close now, amazed at how someone might be able to actually live inside it.

The SUV starts moving then, slowly backing up. Greg supposes it's going to maneuver into The Green's parking area, probably for that Merry Market thing going on this month.

All around the moving shingled house, flurries flutter from the sky. Amidst those spinning flakes, that cute little house is backing down Main Street, right across from his parked sedan, actually.

"Wait." Greg sips his coffee and leans closer to the window. "No …"

He glances up at those flying snowflakes, which *could* be distracting the driver—being that it's the first snowfall of the season. But surely the driver has things under control as the SUV and its towed house continue backing up, inching … inching … inching, closer and closer to his parked car.

As a matter of fact, it's inching too close for comfort. Greg leans to the side and catches a glimpse of the driver. "She's using all her mirrors, I hope," he says to no one in particular as he's riveted to the moving house. Those first flurries fall stronger now, obscuring his view as he takes another bite of his buttered blueberry muffin.

As he has his breakfast snack at his comfortable spot inside the warm coffee shop.

As he watches the world go by through swirling snowflakes, all from his window seat.

"No, no," he whispers then, sipping his coffee and convincing himself his car is safe. "She's got to be watching behind her."

Suddenly Greg sputters into his coffee cup, mid-sip. Because the first tiny house he's *ever* seen in all his livelong days backs straight into—yup—straight into *his* parked car.

"Son of a snowflake!" he mutters as he grabs his coat, stands and hurries outside.

four

"HEY, *HEY*!" GREG CALLS OUT before the coffee shop's door is even closed behind him. He shoves his arms into the sleeves of his long wool coat, all while running toward the curb.

"Oh my gosh," a woman is saying as she steps out of her SUV. "I'm *so* sorry!"

Greg careens to a stop and looks at this petite woman, who appears to be about five feet tall. She's bundled in a shearling-trimmed suede coat looking right out of the 1970s. The woman's straight bangs brush her worried eyes, and Greg thinks … tiny house, driven by—*seriously*? A tiny woman? Then he rushes around his parked car to assess the damage.

"I thought I had clearance to make the turn," this woman is saying as she follows behind him. "My driving record is good. I mean, I even managed the roundabout in this town."

Now *that*? That gets Greg to glance over at her. "Are

30

you okay? You're not hurt, are you?"

"No. No, this was just a little bump-in," she insists while motioning from her house to his sedan. "I was backing up fine, and saw your car in both my mirrors. It is your car, right?" When he nods, she gives him an apologetic smile. "But then this really happy weatherman on the radio said to look up at all the beautiful snow, and, well …" When she stops talking, she just shrugs.

Greg walks around his car to find its rear quarter panel all crumpled in, then looks at the tiny house on its trailer. "Not a scratch on yours."

"I know. But I take full responsibility for the damages. And I'm truly sorry! Here." The woman hands him a business card. "That's my name," she says, leaning close and pointing it out on the card. "And my cell number. My insurance will cover everything, I promise."

Taking the card, Greg reads it closely. Apparently this woman, who looks to be about thirty, runs a business in her tiny house. *Vagabond Vintage*, her card says. *Wherever you roam, you can bring treasures home.* He looks over at the tiny shingled house again, squints through the still-falling snowflakes, then looks back at the card—which he pockets at the same time he takes out his cell phone. Framing the damaged quarter panel in the camera lens, he starts snapping pictures. "I'll need these to submit a claim." Again he looks at this woman. Wait, he missed her name. So he pulls out the business card again. "Lindsey. But I have to hurry, because I really can't be late for work." He moves to the right to snap another angle of the damage.

"I don't think you can drive, though," this mod-looking Lindsey says as she keeps pace with his right-veering, then left-leaning, then back-stepping camera-snapping. "Look!" She points to his deflating rear tire, which a piece of crumpled quarter panel has apparently pierced.

"Oh, swell." This is so not what he needs today, this monkey wrench thrown into his schedule. He swipes out of his phone's camera mode to make a call. "Now I'll need a tow. And I'll definitely be late for work." So with Lindsey hovering close by, he calls his medical office and asks the receptionist to cancel his first few morning appointments.

"Cancel?" she asks.

"I got hit by a house," Greg tells her. He steps off the curb and into the snowy street to take another look at the car's damage.

"I'm so sorry," Lindsey is saying again from behind him while he explains the situation to his office.

Next up? He calls the police, pretty much while ignoring the woman, Lindsey, who caused this fiasco first thing on a Monday morning. "I need to report a traffic accident," he tells the police dispatcher as a layer of fresh-fallen snow covers his car now. "It occurred outside Whole Latte Life, on the corner of Main and Brookside."

"What happened?" the dispatcher asks.

"I got hit by a house."

"A what?"

"A tiny house!" As he says it, Greg turns to examine

the back of Lindsey's house again. How can it not have even a scratch on it?

"Mister … Mister?" Lindsey asks while patting his arm.

"No, *I* didn't get hit," Greg explains to the dispatcher on the phone. "My *car* did. A tiny house backed into my *car.*"

"Oh, mister …"

When he disconnects, Greg backs up a step to grab another photo, then turns to Lindsey. "Davis. Dr. Davis. And I have patients waiting—"

"Dr. Davis. I'm worried." She points to slow-moving traffic passing them. "People are rubbernecking."

"*What?*" From where he stands in the street, Greg squints over his now snow-covered shoulder, through the still-falling snowflakes, at a long line of cars there as drivers gape at the accident. Or, it seems, gape at the endearing, shingled tiny house. "People are *what?*" he repeats.

"Rubbernecking. Trying to see what happened here. They're distracted." Lindsey tugs his arm. "You should move onto the sidewalk, so you don't get hit."

"Okay." Greg follows her onto the sidewalk, then instantly calls the local auto body shop. The owner's a friend of his; surely he'll be able to accommodate Greg.

"Dave's Auto Body," a flustered voice promptly answers.

"Dave, it's Greg Davis. I need a tow," he says into the phone. "I've been hit by a house." As he listens with the phone to his ear, he leans to the side and winces at the sight of his car's damage. "What? No, not a mouse. A *house*. One of those tiny houses. It backed into my car."

"It'll be a few hours," Dave tells him.

"Hours?"

"Oh man, the roundabout is all backed up in this snow flurry. A couple of fender benders right in the middle of it. I'm telling you, Greg, that roundabout is too darn small. People can't maneuver around those tight curves in the snow. Cars are backed up there to kingdom come."

"Seriously?"

"It's madness," Dave insists. "*Pandemonium!*"

"Okay. Well, whenever you can squeeze in my tow." Greg looks long at his dented sedan. "I can't hang around, though, so I'll leave my key under the mat for you."

"Dr. Davis?"

After dialing his father's cell phone next, Greg looks up at Lindsey. She's inched closer—close enough for him to notice the embroidered stitching edging her suede coat's furry cuffs. But he motions for her to wait a sec. "Dad," Greg says into the phone, turning toward his busted car again. He steps off the curb and runs a hand over the snow-covered crumpled quarter panel. "I need a ride to work. Can you swing by?"

"A ride?" Pete asks.

"I'm at Whole Latte Life. I got hit by a house."

"*What?* Are you okay?"

"Yes, yes. My car got hit by one of those tiny houses. It backed into my car, and I need a lift to the office. My appointments are all running late now."

"Dr. Davis? I can—"

Greg holds up a finger while talking to his father. "You can't?" He watches Lindsey turn and go right into her actual house then. She unlocks the door and steps inside!

"No room in the mail truck today, Greg," his father is saying. "It's stuffed to the brim with holiday catalogs and Christmas cards. Already!"

"Okay. Thanks anyway, Dad."

Before he even disconnects, Lindsey emerges from her tiny house. She's tugging on a slouchy, cable-knit visor-beanie, the likes of which Greg hasn't seen in decades.

"Dr. Davis, I can get you—"

But an approaching siren cuts her off. An exasperated police officer arrives on scene. He quickly writes up the accident stats, complaining the whole time about the cars backed up for blocks at *all* entrances to the town's new traffic roundabout. "Horns are blaring," he declares with pen to pad. "Voices yelling out rolled-down windows—"

"Officer," Greg interrupts. "I'm really in a rush."

"Okay, then. Let's get this done. Address?" the cop asks. He jots down Greg's Main Street address, then turns to Lindsey.

"Snowflake Lake," she says. "Temporarily."

"Age?" the officer asks.

"Thirty-five," Greg answers.

Lindsey points to the appropriate space on his clipboarded form. "Thirty-one," she quietly says.

"Occupation?" the officer asks next.

"Business owner." Lindsey motions to her mobile shop. "I run my own boutique-on-wheels, Vagabond Vintage. Oh, I hope my insurance rates don't go up."

"Orthopedic surgeon," Greg cuts in with a frustrated glance at his broken-down car.

At that point, the police officer checks their licenses. Then he jots down notes and arrows indicating the precise angle Lindsey's SUV turned this way, while her trailered tiny house went that way, in the direct path of sedan parked due west—before snapping his clipboard closed. "I've got what I need here," he declares. "Your tow driver will be hours still, if he's going to the roundabout first." The cop takes a closer look at the collision damage. "What a shame." He shakes his head while setting out orange cones behind Greg's car. "Nice luxury sedan and all."

With a sinking feeling, Greg watches the harried cop. Because if there's one thing Greg Davis knows—heck, he can just tell by the police officer's tense tone of voice— it's this: There's no way that cop will give him a lift to work. He's getting in his cruiser, flipping on that siren and driving to one place and one place only: the traffic roundabout, where Greg's sure every cop on the force is now stationed.

Leaving Greg stranded on the sidewalk, where he shoves up the sleeve of his wool coat and checks his watch. "Shoot," he whispers. "And I still need a ride."

"I can drive you."

The voice, well, it's like the voice of an angel swooping

36

in to save his day. Greg's every wish comes true at the sound of those words.

That is, until he turns around and sees precisely who said them.

Sees that petite woman huddled in her visor-beanie and shearling coat. Beneath her long bangs, snow dusts her eyelashes, and her face is flushed with the cold.

"What?" he asks this Lindsey of tiny house fame. Because good grief, even though it's *his* car that got smashed, all he's been hearing from passersby is how cute that little shingled house-on-wheels is.

Lindsey motions to her SUV still pulled over to the curb. "My vehicle's right here and, well, it's awfully available. Jump in?"

Then? Yes, though Greg can't believe it, Lindsey does it. From beneath that slouchy cap where her blonde bangs sweep her face, she gives him a friendly smile while turning up her hands—hands jingling keys that can ultimately get him to his patients.

Greg looks from the hitched tiny house to her SUV, then back at his watch again. "Okay." He takes a quick breath. "Okay, then." A ride's a ride, after all. Any four wheels will get him to work just the same, and that's all that matters.

Lindsey hurries to the driver's door and climbs in just as Greg opens the door on his side, then stops still.

"Come on, get in!" Lindsey says as she turns the key in the ignition. "Oh, just move Santa to the back."

As if Greg Davis' day couldn't get any more surreal, unbelievably, a Santa Claus decoration sits in his seat. A

Santa wearing a long burgundy robe, with a burlap sack slung over his shoulder. After one last sidelong look out at his dinged-up sedan—the one with comfortable padded seats, and whose engine quietly purrs while the sound system plays soft background music—Greg scoops up the old-world Santa. He carefully tucks St. Nick into the crowded-with-boxes backseat of this vehicle hauling a very tiny house … a house that backed smack-dab into Greg's life.

⁓

Rat-a-tat-tat-tat-tat!

Lindsey's arms are loaded with take-out food bags. The aroma drifting from them is enough to have her nearly rip one open and dig in—right here on the front porch of Blue Jay Bungalow.

But she doesn't.

Instead she gives the woodpecker doorknocker another try. *Rat-a-tat-tat-tat!* At the end of a long, tiring day, the least she can do for her uncle Gus is treat him to this delicious dinner. He did pull the right strings, after all, to secure Lindsey's Merry Market business permit. Though she was a little late to her meeting, the folks at town hall were happy to have her tiny house pop-up shop be part of their holiday hodgepodge of boutiques, food trucks, crafters and shops stationed on the town green.

When Gus doesn't answer the door, Lindsey crosses the porch to the window there. Lights are on inside. Old framed photographs are arranged atop her uncle's beloved piano. A few early Christmas cards stand on his mantel.

But no Gus is to be seen.

"Hellooo! Can I help you?" a voice calls out.

Lindsey turns, bags and all, to see a woman in her thirties approaching from the cabin next door. She wears a blue puffy jacket and fluffy earmuffs. "I'm looking for Gus," Lindsey says around her food bags.

"Gus? Gus Haynes?" This lady stops at Blue Jay Bungalow's porch steps. "Can I help you with something? Because I'm pretty sure he has the Holly Trolley shift tonight." She motions vaguely toward where the distant town center might be.

"Oh, no." Lindsey glances straight down at her bags stuffed with warm food, then at the waiting neighbor. "Well. Have *you* eaten?" She smiles apologetically and shifts the bags in her arms. "This was for Gus and me. There's hot chicken cutlets, baked ziti. The works. From Cedar Ridge Tavern. Oh! And I'm Gus' niece, Lindsey!" She tries to extend a hand, but nearly drops a bag when she does.

"Pleased to meet you, Lindsey. I'm Penny. Penny Hart," this Penny-with-copper-colored-hair says as she climbs the porch steps. "Let me take some of those." When she settles a bag in her arms, she looks around it at Lindsey. "Why don't you come over to my place? Cardinal Cabin." Penny hitches her head toward a nearby cabin. "I've got a can of tomato soup heating, to go with a grilled cheese sandwich. But your food sounds way better!"

And so, for the second time in so many days, Lindsey Haynes finds herself in a fairy-tale cabin. In this one, berry wreaths and sprigs of Scotch pine hang from wood-paneled walls. Hooked-wool pillows and soft throws cover the sofa and upholstered chairs. Mason jars etched with cardinal motifs sit on end tables. An antler coatrack is mounted beside the door; logs snap and crackle in a stone fireplace. Beneath a chandelier with white birch-bark shades, pinecones and cinnamon sticks spill from a crystal bowl on the dining room table.

A dining room table to which Penny is now headed.

Lindsey hesitates in the doorway, though, until Penny waves her over. The wonder of it all, of this magical cabin nestled in the pines, is this: It has Lindsey instantly feel like she and Penny are old friends.

In no time, fringed placemats and dinner plates are set out, food doled, and girl-talk ensues as they chatter like, well, like two chickadees. Penny explains how she stayed in Cardinal Cabin last December as a promotional assignment for the travel agency where she works. She had such a special stay, she rented the cabin from Gus for the holidays again this year.

"Come to find out," Penny says with a twinkle in her eye, "old Gus is Snowflake Lake's landlord *and* Christmas Cupid. Last year? He arranged some inadvertent, romantic meetings between me and my boyfriend, Frank. Yes, Gus went and gave us a mistletoe nudge."

"*My* Uncle Gus?" Lindsey asks as she spears a hunk of chicken. "*Cupid?*"

Penny nods. "Frank and I have been together ever since. Gus knew Frank, because, well, Frank helps him out here. You know, chopping wood. Clearing snow. Frank's actually a part-time lumberjack, when he's not busy at the boathouse he and his sister own, on the river."

"Wait. I think I drove by that boathouse. I noticed its big parking lot and wondered about making arrangements to park my tiny house there—temporarily, of course. But that was before I talked to Gus and he insisted I keep it here at the lake."

Penny scoops up a forkful of salad. "Tiny house?" she asks. "You *live* in one? How charming!"

"Oh, sure," Lindsey says, then sips from the wine Penny had poured. "Charming until you back it straight into a local doctor's luxury sedan!"

"No!" Penny stops, squinting at Lindsey across the table. "Wait. A tall doctor, maybe? Light brown hair? Blue eyes?"

Lindsey squints right back at her. On the table, candlelight flickers, setting the silverware and glasses aglow. "Yeah, piercing blue … with a winter chill!"

"Don't tell me it was … Greg Davis? You hit Greg's car?"

Lindsey slowly nods. "This morning, during the snow flurries. I had to maneuver my house into that Merry Market on The Green and got a little distracted by those spinning snowflakes. Which is when I backed right into

Dr. Davis' car parked outside the coffee shop."

"Oh, no."

"Oh, yes. I felt so bad, Penny. But even worse? Apparently the whole town was involved in minor mishaps, so tow truck drivers and taxicabs were all booked. Meaning Dr. Davis couldn't get a ride to his office, where patients were already waiting. Until …"

"You didn't," Penny whispers while waggling an accusing finger at her.

"I did. Guilty as charged. After hitting his car, I actually drove him to work."

"Ooh … Awkward?"

"To say the least." Lindsey explains how her old-world Santa statue had to be jostled about to make room for the good doctor—who'd had just about enough intrusions into his day already. "When we got to the medical complex, Greg put Santa back in the front passenger seat. Where he actually buckled him in! Said we don't need Santa getting hurt in any more fender benders. And the thing is? I couldn't tell if he was still mad about my hitting his car, and being a little sarcastic? Or if he was just being friendly."

"Well," Penny says, lifting a forkful of baked ziti to her mouth. "As long as everyone's safe and sound. What's done is done. As we like to say in this New England town … Water under the covered bridge?" she asks around the food.

Lindsey can only hope. She glances out the paned window of this quaint Cardinal Cabin. Moonlight shines on the pretty little lake outside. The day's earlier snowfall left a lacy white coating on the pine tree branches, on the cabin roofs.

A snow-globe town, indeed.

One that seemed to be given a shake today when a quick and beautiful snow flurry blew into town like a sudden gust of winter wind.

five

NOW THAT HER TINY HOUSE has found a new home for a few weeks at Snowflake Lake, it's time to get to work. First up? A photo shoot for Lindsey's website. She has to announce her latest stop in Addison, Connecticut for the town's Merry Market. This way, her loyal, local customers can visit her shop here—and spread the word.

What better outfit to photograph than a velvet LBD from decades gone by, ideal for the holiday season? She hangs the little black dress with three-quarter sleeves on the dress form she uses to model vintage outfits. After fussing with the dress' button-up turtleneck, she moves the clothed dress form in front of a floor-to-ceiling pleated drape hanging in front of a closet. The cream-colored drape makes a perfect backdrop, and so she snaps two pictures: the dress front and back.

While returning the dress to its hanger, Lindsey glances out the window. Yesterday's snow dusts the ground near the lake, and cardinals chirp in the pine trees surrounding her tiny house. The thing is, that snow-dusted lake would *also* make a perfect backdrop, this time for a winter coat. So she'll showcase her recent find—a 1970s faux-fur jacket with padded shoulders—on the banks of the ice-fringed lake.

As she lifts the fur coat off its hanger, there's a knock at her door.

"Uncle Gus!" Lindsey says, opening the door and waving him inside.

"Lindsey …" Gus steps in and raises an eyebrow at her. "You should've told me."

"Told you? Told you what?" As she asks, she clears some clothing off a tabletop and motions for Gus to have a seat.

"You should've told me *this*." Gus sits and unfolds the *Addison Weekly* newspaper he'd been carrying. He points to the front-page headline: *Local Doctor Hit by a House.*

"Oh." Lindsey slumps into a seat across from Gus. "That."

"Yes! Because I *know* Greg. The good doctor fixed up my old, weary bones after some troublesome wood-chopping. And I could've talked to him, in case the accident caused any ruffled feathers."

"It did." Lindsey slides the paper closer and looks at the photograph of her tiny house behind Greg's perfectly nice, crumpled sedan. "It was awful, Uncle Gus. Even worse, it was the *only* time I've ever gotten into an accident! I was listening to that Leo Sterling talk about the magical first flurries. And how we should look up and take in the exquisite sight of spinning snowflakes. And, well, who doesn't want a bit of magic in their life? So … I did it."

"Did what?"

She shrugs. "I leaned forward and looked up, out through my windshield. But only for a second!" She glances out the window now. "Okay, maybe for two. Because that first flurry *was* magical-looking, I swear. It was like I was right inside the snow globe my father gave me." With that, she stands and retrieves her snowman snow globe from a nearby shelf displaying her cherished collectibles. "And when I was looking up at all those swirling snowflakes, well, I sort of backed into Dr. Davis' car."

Gus takes the snow globe and gives it a flip so its flurries begin. "Hmm. I'm sure Greg understood?" he asks as he sets down the globe. "He's a reasonable person. Very calm … and practical. You know, in that doctorly way."

"I'm not so sure." Lindsey lifts the newspaper and scrutinizes the picture of Dr. Gregory Davis standing in his long wool coat, caught pacing while on his cell phone. "Anyway, I don't think he'll like seeing this and reliving the moment. Because, well, I *did* give him a ride to work afterward, and he wasn't too happy. At all."

"Is that so?"

"Oh, yes," Lindsey sighs. "And all on my account." She folds the newspaper in half and slides it back across the tabletop.

"You keep that," Gus says.

Wait. Lindsey squints suspiciously at Gus. Was there a

twinkle in his eye as he said that? Did he actually bring over the paper so that she can read up on this Dr. Davis, who everyone around here seems to like?

"Yes, keep it. You know," Gus quickly adds. "So you can … check out the town's holiday events. Yes, that's it." He stands then and puts on his tweed wool cap. "I've got some errands to run now, and have to stop at Chuck's Chicken for a sandwich, too, before my trolley shift."

"Wait, Uncle Gus," Lindsey says, following him to the door. "Do you have a minute?" As she asks, she's slipping her arms into the faux-fur jacket. "Because I need to get a picture taken for my online shop."

"Picture?" Gus looks back over his shoulder.

Lindsey nods and gives a twirl in her waist-length furry swing jacket.

Ten minutes later, it's done. She poses lakeside for the picture she wanted for her shop's website. But Lindsey not only poses, she also makes the scene *holiday*-related for her online customers.

Which is easy enough to accomplish, thanks to one recent roadside treasure she'd found. Yes, she carried her old-world Santa outside, too, and stood him near the lake. Now, a cold breeze ruffles his long burgundy coat as she straightens the stocking cap on his head. Something about this old-fashioned cabin community frozen in time suits the shot she has in mind.

After Gus angles the camera to include one of those charming cabins in the background, Lindsey strikes her pose, wearing the waist-length, faux-fur coat.

As though she's revealing her very own secret Christmas wish, Lindsey leans close, cups her hand to her mouth and whispers in Santa's ear—just as Gus gets the shot.

❧

Greg knows.

As soon as two mail trucks peel into the lot at Dave's Auto Body Shop, it's obvious. His father and brother have read every stinking detail of the doctor getting hit by a house.

Because yes, today is Tuesday: *Addison Weekly* delivery day. Their mail trucks must be loaded down with the story of the sorry doctor. And now they tracked him down, never to let up on his troubles. Greg stands there and simply turns up his hands at the two mailmen.

"Called your office," his brother, Wes, says as he rushes over and shakes Greg's hand. "They said you'd be here to check on your car. Is it totaled, guy?"

"What? Totaled? No, just—"

"You're front-page news, son!" Pete yells as he gets out of his mail truck, all while waving a copy of the paper. "When you told me about this yesterday, I didn't think it was *this* big."

Greg snatches the paper and rereads the headline that's all but burned into his memory: *Local Doctor Hit by a House.* "Sufferin' snowflakes," he mutters, then tosses the paper back to his father and heads across the parking lot.

48

"Seriously, Scrubs?" Wes asks while tagging along beside him. "You made the front page because you were hit by a *house*? I've got to see the damages. Where's your car?"

Greg hitches his head to the side lot. On the way there, they pass plenty of other cars with bent fenders, dinged doors, heaved hoods. Yesterday's first flurries left a deluge of destruction in their wake.

"Hey, Doc!" a voice calls out.

Greg looks over to see the auto body shop owner, Dave, approaching.

"That house clipped you good," Dave tells him.

"Yeah, and I need those wheels to get to work," Greg says as they walk toward his sedan with the crumpled quarter panel. "Can you fix my car anytime soon?"

"Heck, no. Wish I had better news for you, but my lot's overflowing with fender benders. Especially from in that snowy roundabout. Folks just couldn't maneuver it."

"No kidding," Pete says, catching up with them. "I've seen cars pull a real no-no and come to a dead stop there, just to let someone merge in. Nearly drove right into them."

"That's nothing," Wes counters. "Last week, a pedestrian stopped me in my mail truck, right in the middle of the roundabout—waved me down with a letter to mail! Said I saved him a trip to the post office. Then he even wanted to know if I sold stamps off the truck."

"Are you kidding me?" Pete asks. "Now that one takes the cake."

"Yup. Lots of horn honking happened during *that* exchange." Wes nears Greg's car and runs a hand over the dented metal. "It's *crazy* in that roundabout, I'm telling you."

"Looks pretty bad, son," Pete says, eyeing the damaged sedan now.

"It is. So I need a vehicle to get around in while mine's in the shop. I can't be calling a taxi every time I go to the hospital." Or, he thinks while remembering his ride yesterday, can't be expecting a certain woman, towing her tiny house, to give him a lift. "Dave, do you have any rentals available? Something short-term?"

"Nope." Dave stands there, arms crossed, and gives a shrug. "Cleaned out yesterday, after that snow squall. All I've got left are a few used cars for sale."

"Really ..." Greg hikes up the collar of his long wool coat. "You *sell* cars, too?"

"Sure," Dave tells him. "I do a lot of restoration. Come on, I'll show you fellas."

Dave now leads the way to a corner of the parking lot strung with red, yellow and green plastic flags. They flip and flap in the chill breeze.

"Look at this one," Wes says, stopping in front of a dependable, four-wheel drive SUV. "Nice and safe." He looks over at Greg. "Reliable."

"I was *driving* safe and reliable. My sedan is silver, and statistically silver is the safest car." Greg walks past Wes' reliable choice. "And look what happened to it."

"Son?" Pete asks as he pulls down the earflaps of his regulation postal-carrier hat. "Now think about this. You have a respectable position in town. Maybe just wait for your car to be repaired before you do something drastic."

"I think I'm ready for a change, Dad." Greg turns to Dave. "Do you take trades?"

"Absolutely."

"Okay, then. Fix up my sedan and you can sell it. Because I'm trading it in."

Instead of hearing some backfiring, sputtering arguments from his brother and father, surprisingly the men go silent. But Greg catches them elbowing each other, and sees Pete motioning Wes toward an apple-red pickup truck.

Wes hurries to its driver's door, then runs his hand along the side of the truck bed. "Hey, Scrubs. Look at this truck. Just like mine, man. You can haul stuff, bags of dirt. Mulch."

"I live in a condo. What do I need to haul dirt for?" Greg asks.

"Well, how about this van?" Pete asks as he slides open the side door to a family van. He peers longingly inside, saying, "You can fill it up with grandkids. A junior whittler, maybe." He slams the van door shut and turns to Wes and Greg. "Come on, sons. Where are my little grandbucks?"

As his father and brother debate the merits of a family van over a full-size pickup, Greg wanders off. His eye is drawn to another vehicle, over on the side. As he walks to it, a thought runs through his mind, almost like a song stuck in his head. It's the tagline of that Lindsey's vintage shop, words he read on her business card: *Wherever you roam, you can bring treasures home.*

Huddled in his long wool coat, Greg thinks that *he* certainly hasn't brought any treasures home. Here it is another Christmas, and another year of being alone.

So. So maybe you have to *roam* to find the treasures. He approaches the black car that's grabbed hold of his attention.

Yeah, maybe you have to roam ... like a mustang.

He pictures a lone mustang charging out in the wild, its mane flying, its head reared.

Freedom.

Heck, freedom from women, freedom from ties.

That's Greg, all right. Unattached like the wild mustang.

While standing beside *this* bad black Mustang on the used-car lot, Greg turns and calls to Dave, "I'll take this one."

Decision made.

As if to prove it, he opens the door of the 1968 Mustang Fastback and settles in the driver's seat. His gloved hands grip the steering wheel; his gaze looks out the windshield and pictures an open road before him.

"That's a sweet one," Dave says. With a hand on the car's roof, he leans in and points out the original black dashboard with glimmering silver-rimmed gauges; the chrome dials and black push buttons on the AM/FM radio. "Just finished fully restoring her. She's got a new front end, new exhaust system, new paint."

"No kidding." Greg gives the steering wheel a nudge.

"Rack-and-pinion steering. And best of all? A V8 under the hood. Purrs like a—well, more like … growls like a lion."

Greg lets out a low whistle as he looks over at the passenger seat, then twists to get a glimpse of the impeccably restored backseat area, too: the new black carpeting and pleated, black vinyl seats; the silver-trimmed crank windows.

Suddenly, that passenger door swings open and his father leans in. "Son?" he asks. "What's gotten into you? This will have no traction on snowy roads!"

"Dad. I drive from my condo, to the medical office, to the hospital. I basically circle around town, over and over." Greg adjusts the rearview mirror, already feeling possessive of the sleek automobile. "My life's like a perpetual roundabout."

Wes leans in on the passenger side, too. He flips the front seat forward and scopes out the back. "It's got a decent trunk, but not much room here, Scrubs. For all your work gear."

"No, it's good. It suits the new me," Greg tells him while setting his hands on the steering wheel again to get a feel for this fully refurbished mean machine.

"The *new* you?" Wes asks.

"Right," Greg tells him. "Because I'm no longer a luxury sedan kind of man."

Pete comes around to the driver's side, bends low and peers inside, suspiciously eyeing Greg in the driver's seat. "Son?" he asks again.

six

DARN IT IF HIS FATHER wasn't right.

On Greg's way to work the next morning, his Mustang fishtails while he maneuvers through the town roundabout. All it took to slicken the pavement was a light dusting of snow that fell overnight.

Or, heck, more likely it's that *and* the V8 engine chomping at the bit beneath the car's hood.

Okay, then. Maybe his father wasn't so off his nut after all, saying a sports car will have no traction on snowy roads. Because on Greg's first Mustang ride, it feels more like he's riding a buckin' bronco.

"Got to tame this beast," Greg whispers, letting up on the gas when the fishtail begins.

So he downshifts, shimmies to the right, and keeps shimmying straight out of the traffic roundabout. A roundabout in which—he duly noted earlier—all incoming vehicles came to a stop to watch the lone black Mustang rumble through it.

Now he keeps going with a sigh of relief and a brief glance back in his rearview mirror. Oh, and he does one more thing, especially while listening to the weather forecast on the radio.

He makes a mental note: Get snow tires.

Studded snow tires.

⟨∾⟩

"I've never been on a snowtorcycle before!" Lindsey exclaims. She's sitting in the sidecar of Gus' snazzy, squat motorcycle. The sidecar has a windshield, safety bar and comfortable padded seat, where she sits as Gus putt-putts through town. But it's the snowtorcycle's fat, all-terrain tires that get Gus through snow, rain, sleet or shine.

"Glad to give you a ride," Gus calls over to her. "It's very safe-going in the snow. And you have lots of packages to deliver there."

As they idle at a traffic light, Lindsey tells him about the untold orders she's getting from her lakeside photo shoots. She lifts one package, half-shouting, "Suede gloves for a woman in Montana." Lifting another wrapped-and-addressed box, she adds, "A 1950s clutch to a lady in Illinois. My customers love the lake scenery. I even had Penny's fella, Frank, model a hat and scarf for me at his chopping block. He held the axe, split a log, and the picture was so nice, the scarf and hat sold right away!"

With a nod and a slight rev, Gus accelerates when the light changes. He slows, though, when a black Mustang approaches and swerves a little on the slushy road.

"What fool drives a sports car in the snow?" Gus calls to Lindsey over the sputtering snowtorcycle engine. "They're not built for winter driving!"

Lindsey looks back at the passing vintage car. It's jet black, with lots of shiny silver chrome—the bumpers, mirrors, door trim. A true classic like that would be so rad in a photo shoot. Fun images run through her mind … She could model some 1960s mod wool cape and lace-up knee-high boots while standing beside that old sports car. The next pose? One of her opening the driver's door, about to get in. She gives another glimpse over her shoulder just as Gus turns into the post office. The parking lot is already filled, even this early in the day.

"People must be sending lots of Christmas cards and gifts," Lindsey says to Gus as she climbs out of the snowtorcycle, grabs up all her packages until they're tottering in her arms, then heads inside. "I'll try not to be too long!" she calls before hurrying across the parking lot as a young man holds the post office door open for her.

❧

Greg can't help it. He knows it's not the cool thing to do, but whatever. He cuts himself some slack after parking in the medical center's lot. This *new* Greg Davis grabs his lab coat and bag, then swings the Mustang door shut and starts to walk across the parking lot.

That's when he does it.

Yup. He looks over his shoulder at the meanest 'stang around, still not believing it's all his. Seriously, he has to *see* it to convince himself. At least for a day or two. Then, well, by then he'll be nonchalant enough with his new identity to *not* look back at his own boss vehicle. He'll just walk away as if it's simply natural that someone like himself owns the baddest car in town.

He even sneaks in one more look before opening the door to the medical building, then finds himself whistling a tune up the elevator. Still whistling, he walks down the hall to his practice.

"Oh! Dr. Davis," the receptionist calls out upon spotting him. "Phone call."

With his lab coat—that's right, unironed—slung over his arm, Greg keeps walking toward his office. "Who is it?" he asks. "Can you take a message?"

"But it's Gus!" the receptionist insists. "Gus Haynes."

"Okay, fine." Greg turns back and tells her, "I'll take it at my desk." Headed to his office again, he gives his car keys a jangle while he walks.

"Dr. Davis?"

Greg slows and looks back at the receptionist. She's leaning across her own desktop and squinting down the hall at him.

"You seem … *different* today," she says. "Nice to see some pep in your step!"

He looks at her for a moment, nods, then opens his office door. After hanging his slightly wrinkled lab coat on a chair back, he first glances out toward the receptionist area, thinking … *Different?* With a shrug, he picks up the phone.

"Gus, my man. How are you?"

"Okay enough to get around. I'm at the post office right now. But that darn rotator cuff's been acting up. Ever since I split a log or two when Frank couldn't make it to the cabins. Any chance you can check out my arm, be sure I didn't do some mini-minor damage?"

Greg glances at his overbooked desk calendar. "Lunchtime work for you? Can you swing by my office?"

"Might have to cover the Holly Trolley for a couple of hours today. Then I have to fill the bird feeders, *if* I can lift my arm high enough. You know I like to keep those feeders brimming for the cardinals at the lake."

Greg takes a long breath and checks his watch. "How about later this afternoon? I'll make a house call and stop by your place when I'm done here."

"Okay. That works for me."

Greg hears Gus say a quick hello to someone familiar he must see at the undoubtedly busy post office.

"And you'll stay for dinner, too," Gus tells Greg as he starts up his snowtorcycle engine. Its sputtering *putt-putt* sound comes through the phone. "I'll cook us something good and we'll catch up, you and I."

❧

"Sorry it took so long," Lindsey says as she climbs into the snowtorcycle's sidecar. "Service was really slow. But with my arms full, a polite gentleman did offer to hold my packages."

"Is that right?" Gus asks while tipping up the brim of his tweed newsboy cap, then revving the idling engine.

Lindsey nods. "Brian. He was very friendly. We had a nice chat, waiting in line."

As soon as she settles in, Gus accelerates his fancy snow-bike with a little jolt. They cruise down Riverside Drive, where he points out the Addison Boathouse. It's fully decorated for the season: twinkling lights strung along the roofline, wreaths on the grand doorways, garland wound up nearby lampposts.

When they get to the end of Brookside Road, headed back to Snowflake Lake, the old covered bridge comes into sight. Gus' snowtorcycle putters across, its fat tires thunking over the planked floor.

Finally, at the end of Old Willow Road, they turn off onto the one-lane path through the woods. In no time, they're stopped at the doorway to Lindsey's tiny house beside Snowflake Lake.

"Thanks, Uncle Gus!" she says as she steps out. "I didn't have to unhitch my SUV this way, so you saved me some time."

Gus nods and lifts his cap. "Listen, Lindsey," he says, craning from his padded seat as she unlocks her tiny house door. "You come for dinner tonight, why don't you?" he calls over the sputtering snowtorcycle engine. "I'm trying a new recipe and it's no fun sampling it alone."

"Oh. That sounds great." She steps closer and raises

her voice. "But are you sure it's not too much?"

"No, I like to tinker in the kitchen. And we'll catch up on all the family gossip."

"I'll bring dessert, then. Let's see …" she sort of yells, finger tapping her chin. "Frosted chocolate-chip cookies sound good?"

Giving a nod, Gus revs his snowtorcycle before whooshing around the lake toward Blue Jay Bungalow—tooting the horn as he goes.

seven

GREG HASN'T BEEN OUT TO Snowflake Lake in a while. Not since last winter, as a matter of fact, when he brought a Christmas care basket to Penny Hart at Cardinal Cabin. Ah yes, being here at this cabin community tonight is another cruel reminder of his near brush with romance. Without a doubt, that's been the story of his recent life. Near brushes. Passing glances. Wishful thinking.

Well, he's having none of that this year. His hopeful holiday heart has been shelved; any romance attempts, benched. Instead, this holiday, he's the new solidly single Greg Davis.

Just him and his Mustang. A man and his car.

Together, they rumble into Snowflake Lake's little parking area in twilight's shadows. Minutes later, Greg walks in the late-afternoon darkness directly to Gus' Blue Jay Bungalow.

Tunnel vision, yes, that's what he has tonight as he crosses the narrow path. No glancing around at the lake—

ideal for moonlit walks. No taking in the sight of the soaring, twinkling lakeside Christmas tree—perfect for hanging a special ornament on, *with* someone special. No wistful sighs at the vision of smoke curling from all the cabins' chimneys beneath the starlit sky—smoke from fireplaces meant to snuggle in front of.

No, instead this new Greg Davis stamps his slushers on Gus' doormat and gives the woodpecker doorknocker a *rat-a-tat-tat-tat!* This is pretty much a simple house call, after all, with a quick dinner thrown in the mix. When he hears Gus' raised voice yell from inside to come on in, Greg opens the door.

"Smells good," Greg says as he sets down the bag he'd been holding and rubs his gloved hands together to warm up. "What's cooking?"

"Spaghetti and meatballs," Gus answers from the kitchen.

"Excellent." A roaring fire crackles in the stone fireplace. Greg crosses the wood-planked floor toward the flames' warmth. Early Christmas cards line the mantel, and framed family photographs on a lace runner cover the top of a piano at the side wall. Turning back toward Gus in the kitchen, Greg adds, "I stopped at SaveRite and bought a loaf of fresh garlic bread."

"I'll melt some butter, then. It'll be good on the slices."

As he slips out of his long wool coat, Greg leans toward the kitchen to see Gus cooking at the stove. "Now how's that rotator cuff? Want me to check it out before dinner?"

"I'm busy right now." Gus sets down a wooden spoon

and extends his arm, then moves it in slow, wide circles. "A little sore when I raise it."

"You resting?" Greg asks when he hooks his black coat on the antler coatrack beside the door.

"Yessiree."

"Eating right?" Greg tucks his leather gloves into the coat pockets. "To stay strong?"

"Always."

"Still have the printout of exercises I gave you to try last time?"

"I do. Started them this morning after I called you. Did some of those doorway stretches to loosen up, first."

"Okay, good," Greg says as he walks to the dining room sideboard and grabs a platter for his loaf of garlic bread. "If that shoulder's not feeling better by Monday, you call me and I'll give it a thorough exam in my office." The birch-bark chandelier glows over the table as he sets the platter there. Sets it there while noticing not two place settings, but three. All three nicely arranged on plaid placemats, each with a wine goblet, linen napkin and silver flatware, too. "Expecting someone else?" Greg asks.

"As a matter of fact ..." Gus says from the kitchen, just as the doorknocker interrupts.

Rat-a-tat-tat-tat-tat!

⌒∾◯

"Uncle Gus?" Lindsey calls out when she opens the door, not waiting for Gus to answer it.

"In here!" Gus' voice comes from the kitchen.

"I brought those cookies like I promised!" she says, sweeping into the warm cabin, then turning to shut the door behind her. "How do chocolate-dipped chocolate-chip cookies with snowflake sprinkles sound?"

"*Uncle* Gus?" another voice interrupts.

Not her uncle's voice. But clearly a man's voice, one vaguely familiar.

One that has Lindsey spin around so quickly, her wool-brimmed beanie falls off her head. There, standing beside the dining table, is Greg—wearing a zip-up cardigan and button-down shirt over black pants. "Oh! Dr. Davis!" She picks up her hat and fumbles with it.

"What are *you* doing here?" they both ask at the same time.

"I'm here for dinner," Lindsey explains. "Gus is my uncle. My father's brother." Lindsey crosses the living room and sets her cookie container beside a wicker rooster on the dining room sideboard.

"Don't take off your coat, Lindsey." Gus stands in the kitchen doorway as he cups a spaghetti-sauce-dripping wooden spoon.

"Why? Are we going out somewhere?" she asks, then walks over and manages a hug around the sauce spoon.

"No. I just put on the pasta. Maybe while it's cooking, you and Greg can string the rest of my Christmas lights on the front porch? My rotator cuff's been bothering me—"

"Oh no! Are you okay?"

Gus nods. "I'll be fine, Lindsey. Greg's here on a house call to check it out, just to be sure. But I couldn't reach up and finish hanging all those lights."

"Well, I'd be happy to." Lindsey turns to Greg. "I love twinkly lights," she says, just as he's shoving his arms into the sleeves of his long wool coat. While buttoning it up, he opens the door and motions her through.

Out on the porch, the air is cold, the evening quiet beside the lake. The moon is just rising, casting faint illumination on the water, which is fringed with wild grasses covered with silver frost.

"I want to tell you again that I'm very sorry, Greg. About backing into your car the other day." Lindsey picks up a string of lights from the porch railing. "And I hope you're not mad."

"Eh," he answers while sorting a half-hung string of lights left dangling. He picks up the end of the strand and loops it over a few hooks. "You ended up doing me a favor, anyway."

"A favor?"

"Yeah. I went and traded in that boring sedan for something with more soul. A '68 Mustang, actually."

"Really! Wow." She pauses, tipping her head and squinting at him while trying to remember the driver of the old Mustang she'd seen in town earlier as it swerved on the slippery roads. "This morning, were you …"

"Was I what?"

She still squints, then shakes her head with a small smile. "I mean, will it be okay in the snow?"

"I'll manage," he says, stretching up to the porch roofline, but not quite reaching the light hooks there. "I just need the right snow tires. And ..." he says while hurrying across the porch. "And this footstool." He sets it firmly beneath the half-strung lights and steps up on it. "That's better."

They don't say much then. Just a *Careful!* here, and a *Hand me another strand* there, as—little by little—Blue Jay Bungalow is strung with white lights. They sidestep two slatted-wood rockers; and a big basket stuffed with split logs for the fireplace; and a tall, metal lantern aglow with a flickering candle. Every few feet, Greg steps down and slides over the footstool, and Lindsey moves along with him while holding a ball of tangled lights in her hands. As the shadow of tall pines rises around them, a cold breeze picks up and rustles the tree branches ... the hush merely a whisper beneath the twinkling lights of the cozy cabin's porch.

~

Standing out there in the cold night air did one thing for certain: It worked up a hardy appetite, one well-suited to spaghetti and meatballs. Lindsey's not sure she's ever eaten a more delicious plate of pasta.

"Uncle Gus, your sauce is, well, it's garlic-bread-draggin'-good," she says while swiping a hunk of buttered bread through the dregs of sauce on her plate.

"Hear, hear," Greg adds, raising his garlic bread in a toast.

66

"Glad you both like it, especially after you finished my porch-decorating for me," Gus tells them as he spears half a meatball on his fork.

"We actually see a big increase in injuries at the hospital this merry time of year," Greg says. "Lots of folks hurt themselves decorating for the holidays."

"Really!" Lindsey bites off a mouthful of her sauce-soaked, buttered bread.

Nodding, Greg continues. "They fall off the roof while setting decorations up there. Or slip off ladders while hanging lights on their gutters. Even putting the stars on trees! You'd be amazed at how many people lose their balance and grab onto the tree, which then crashes onto them and breaks a rib—or they fracture a wrist in their fall."

"Oh my gosh! 'Tis your busy season, then." Lindsey gazes around her uncle's cabin, at the wood-paneled walls and roaring fireplace. A tin bucket brimming with large pinecones sits on the hearth. "Now that I have a place to stay for the holiday season, I'd like to string some lights on my tiny house, too. Just a *tiny* bit," Lindsey tells them with a wink. "Maybe around the doorway, and I'll try not to slip off my step stool and end up in the hospital."

"You really *live* in that little house?" Greg leans back and eyes her. "I mean, full time?"

"I do."

"There's not a bigger home base somewhere?" Greg asks, turning back his cardigan cuffs. "For when you're not on the road?"

"Nope." Lindsey tucks her hair behind an ear and considers how to explain her tiny life in her tiny house. "That little shingled house is my tiny home, sweet home. It's my business, too. My vintage clothing boutique fits snug as a bug inside it. And what I like best about it all is that I'm self-sufficient *and* self-contained. There's a freedom to that. I mean, I'm free to roam, even while ... staying home. Like now," she says, reaching over and clasping her uncle's hand. "I never expected to be parking here this month for Addison's Merry Market, *and* visiting with my uncle. But here I am, and all because of my tiny house."

"I put in a phone call to push through some paperwork," Gus explains to Greg then. "Lindsey's shop, Vagabond Vintage, will be on The Green several evenings every week."

"You'll drive your house ... right there?" Greg asks, his meatball-laden fork hovering.

Lindsey nods. "Oh, and Uncle Gus! Did you know that *Greg* bought a new car?"

"You did?" Gus asks, his elbows on the table now.

Greg nods. "Traded in the luxury sedan—"

"For a vintage *Mustang*!" Lindsey adds with a knowing wink at her uncle. Surely he'll remember the slip-sliding Mustang they witnessed this morning on their way to the post office.

"Is that right ..." Gus reaches for the wine bottle and adds a splash to his glass. "And how's she handle, Greg? That Mustang of yours."

"A little like a wild horse, I'll tell you," Greg explains.

"Has a lot of muscle under the hood and I have to rein her in sometimes."

While patting his mouth with a napkin, Gus stands and scoops up his dinner plate. "Well I'll be darned. Never thought I'd see you driving a hot rod like that."

"Oh, Uncle Gus! Let me clean the dishes," Lindsey insists, picking up her own fork and knife.

"No, no. This is easy work." He turns back and hitches his head toward the living room. "You two can help me out another way. Over at that table by the window."

Greg tips back in his chair for a better look. "The one with puzzle boxes on it?"

"That's right. Every year, I put together a Christmas puzzle special for my grandkids. We frame it and they take it home as a keepsake. Be nice if the two of you picked out this year's puzzle. My family will be here Christmas Eve." Gus carries a couple of plates into the kitchen, calling back, "Anyway, there's three boxes there. Choose one the children might like."

⌒◞◟◞◠◠

The problem, though, isn't the puzzles.

No. The problem is getting *to* those puzzles. First, Greg and Lindsey nearly collide when they leave the dining room table to head for the living room. Then, when Greg turns back to push in Lindsey's chair, she inadvertently does the same, at the same moment—so they bump hands, then quickly step back. Both motion for the other to go ahead, and when they laugh and take a step, it's in an uncomfortable unison once more as they nearly bump. Again.

Finally, they make it to the living room.

Each sits on either side of the puzzle table.

And their knees knock, prompting Greg to clear his throat and back up his chair.

At last, puzzle decision-time is at hand. The choice is between either Santa checking his gift list near a fireplace; or a woodland landscape where deer and raccoons and a snowman string garland and hang ornaments on a snowy pine tree; or a scene of cardinals perched on a snow-laden mailbox outside a festively decorated cabin nestled in snowy hills.

After much hemming and hawing over the merits of each picturesque puzzle, they're at a stalemate.

Until Lindsey has an idea.

"On the count of three," she says while spreading the puzzle boxes across the tabletop, "we'll each point to the one we want. If it's the same one, *that's* the Christmas puzzle Gus will put together."

"Okay," Greg says, barely inching his chair closer to the table—as though he's afraid they'll bump knees or elbows or *something* again.

"One," Lindsey whispers.

They both shift in their seats.

"Two," Greg says.

Lindsey sits up perfectly straight. "And, three!"

In a blur, they both point. And both entangle their

arms all crisscrossed over the other.

"Oops," Lindsey quietly says while trying to extricate hers from his.

The thing is, it happens at the same time that Greg lowers, then raises his arm off hers. "Well, look at that," he says, straightening his wristwatch. "I lost track of time, and have an early shift at the hospital tomorrow."

"Really?" Lindsey asks.

"My turn for morning rounds," Greg says from the antler coatrack, where he's lifting off his long black coat. "Got to hit the road, Gus," he calls out while slipping into the sleeves.

"But what about Lindsey's cookies with cocoa?" Gus asks. He hurries out of the kitchen while drying his hands on a towel.

"Cookies-to-go tonight, unfortunately. Work calls." Greg hikes his coat up higher around his shoulders.

"I'm pretty tired myself, after all that cooking." Gus looks from Lindsey to Greg. "*And* after hurting that problematic rotator cuff." As he says it, he slightly moves his arm in a circular motion. "Think I'll turn in early."

The cabin fills with an awkward silence then. One that Lindsey felt right along, bumping into Greg all evening. So she gets up from the puzzle table, grabs her coat and hugs her uncle. "You have a cookie with warm milk," she tells him. "Your arm will feel better in no time. Cookies always work like magic!"

"Feel free to take some for yourself, Lindsey. And for Greg, too."

"I think I'll do just that, Uncle Gus." After wrapping a plate of cookies, she heads to the cabin door and pulls on her brimmed beanie.

Gus follows, stopping at the puzzle table and having a seat there. "Wait up, kids! Which puzzle did you decide on?"

Lindsey turns back to point one out, yup, at the same time Greg does, causing another inadvertent minor mini-collision.

"Sorry," Greg quietly says, backing up a step.

Lindsey nods and quickly picks a puzzle, any puzzle, just to be on her way and extricated from this man who's been so tangled up in her direct path recently. As she points out the cardinals-on-the-mailbox puzzle, she bends and leaves a whispered *Goodnight* and quick kiss on her uncle's cheek, before hurrying for the door.

Greg gives a wave to Gus, then opens the door for Lindsey. But after the endless run-ins they just had inside Blue Jay Bungalow, she cautiously steps back until he gives her the nod that all's clear.

"Now Greg," Gus calls from his seat at the puzzle table, where he's already opening the cardinal puzzle box. "You be sure to walk Lindsey home."

While pulling on his leather gloves, Greg looks over from the doorway.

"Oh, that's okay." Still clutching the cookie plate, Lindsey pokes her head back inside the cabin. "I don't want to be a bother."

"Nonsense. You two are both leaving, so you should

walk together." Gus goes to the fireplace and picks up a flickering lantern from the hearth. "And it's dark, so take this. It'll light the way to her tiny house."

Greg happens to be bent over tightening his slush-shoes, so Lindsey reaches for the lantern—at the precise moment Greg straightens and, that's right, bumps her arm, too.

When they untangle again, Greg takes the lantern and motions for Lindsey to go ahead, out to the porch. *Goodnights* are called out once more, and the front door closed against the cold before Lindsey walks down the few porch steps.

Which is when everything comes together. Everything about the night.

Well, about her uncle Gus and his … Cupid ways.

Because when she looks back, there's Gus sitting in the lamplit window at the puzzle table. He's watching them leave.

And, if Lindsey's not mistaken, there's a merry twinkle in his eye as he raises a bushy white eyebrow, winks and gives a wave.

༄

It's more of the same old, same old.

The thought doesn't leave Greg as he walks beside Lindsey on the way to her tiny house nestled lakeside.

Yes, as he listens to Lindsey making small talk, the plate of wrapped cookies in her hands, it's déjà vu. It's his life on repeat. Whatever you want to call it, he's been here, done that.

Heck, it was only last December when he walked around this very lake. Walked with pretty Penny Hart beside him.

And then had his holiday heart broken, for the third straight year in a row.

So it won't happen again, no way, no how. Oh, he'll politely go through the motions and get Lindsey safely home.

But that's it.

There will be no romantic thoughts. No wondering if he should ask her out on a date. No giving a compliment that she looked nice tonight in her high-waisted corduroy bell bottoms, topped with a chunky Fair Isle sweater. No brushing a strand of her straight blonde bangs from her eyes as he whispers, *Goodnight*.

Nothing.

Because if there's one thing Greg Davis knows, it's this: Trying leads to nothing. No matter how much he might be fooled by a gentle smile. By a grazing touch on his arm.

"I'm over there, parked between the two pine trees," Lindsey says, pointing through the long shadows beneath the December moon. "Uncle Gus thought it was a nice serene spot to land my house for a bit. Not to mention, electrical and water hookups are available as part of the lake's small RV area."

Greg simply nods and holds the lantern up higher to

light the way. Lindsey's tiny home is only a short distance from Blue Jay Bungalow, and they get to her doorstep in no time.

"Can you hold the light closer?" she asks while putting her key in the door lock. "It's a little dark and I can't really see."

Greg walks up behind her and raises the lantern again. When she unlocks the door and pushes it open, she turns quickly and bumps right into the lantern.

"Oh!" Lindsey backs up a step. "Sorry." A quick smile, then, "We always seem to be colliding," she says.

"No problem. Here, you keep the lantern." He sets it down at her doorstep. "That way you can return it to Gus."

"Are you sure?"

"I'll find my way to my car." Greg turns to leave. "Maybe I'll see you around," he calls over his shoulder.

"Oh, wait!" Lindsey says. "These are yours. I have extra inside."

Greg looks back, hesitates, then meets her halfway and takes the plate of wrapped cookies, almost dropping it in the clumsy exchange. "Thanks, Lindsey," he says before turning and walking into the shadows, just him and his cookies now.

Him and his cookies, headed to his rogue Mustang.

In the past, the old Greg Davis would've looked back at Lindsey. Would've given a friendly second wave.

Not this time.

Nope, not the new Greg Davis, who recently vowed

with three darts to stop trying.

Tossed three darts in Joel's Bar and Grille, while solemnly swearing off any holiday hunt for romance.

No, in the dark woods, Greg walks alone in his wool coat and dependable slusher shoes. It's best this way: no risk, no pain. Instead, he keeps his head up and charges forward without a glance back.

Without even a *bit* of wondering.

eight

A FEW DAYS LATER, IT begins.

That's what Greg thinks Saturday afternoon with a glance at the wall calendar in his condo. The first of untold holiday parties, gatherings and festivities gets underway in just hours. Oh, it's here ... the season of dinners and laughs, of mingling and caroling—all beneath swags of garland, beside Christmas trees, while candles glimmer and white lights shimmer.

Quickly pulling on a cashmere sweater over his button-down shirt, he grabs his black wool coat and key ring before rushing out the door. It's not until he's tossed his coat in the back and is seated in his Mustang that he remembers the Secret Santa gift.

That is, the gift he has yet to buy.

Easy enough to remedy, though. All it takes is a mile or so drive down Main Street. His Mustang rumbles past little shops a-twinklin'; past Dutch colonials and Federals adorned with balsam wreaths—their burgundy bows fluttering in the cold breeze. When he veers into Snowflakes and Coffee Cakes' parking lot right beside Addison Cove, it strikes him that the *old* Greg Davis would've bought a Secret Santa gift weeks ago. *That* present would already be wrapped and ribboned, with just the right greeting card attached.

In the late-afternoon light, he checks his reflection in the rearview mirror, drags a hand across his jaw. "That old Greg Davis would've shaved, too," he says to himself.

Instead, the *new* Greg Davis—shadow of whiskers and all—rushes into the grand old Christmas barn. He's a little panicked while looking up at the loft as a model train chugs around an elaborate ceramic Christmas village. It's a miniature town remarkably like Addison itself, where paned windows glow in homes and chapels; where passersby dressed in scarves and mittens peer into frosty shop display windows; where rooftops and pine boughs are snowcapped; where rosy-cheeked carolers stand—songbooks in hand, faces tipped up in song.

Elsewhere in the barn, large gold snowflakes hang from rough-hewn rafters; decorative wrapped gifts spill from sleighs; ornaments of red and gold hang from wall displays; nutcrackers cover round tables; trees of every size sparkle and twinkle beneath dangling icicles and tiny lights.

And in a sudden blur, Jingles, the store cat, bats a wayward jingle bell across the wood-planked floor.

"Greg! Why you're all dressed up," shop owner Vera Sterling says as she approaches. Her blonde hair hangs in a loose side braid, and she wears a beige fisherman sweater over her jeans. "Looking awfully dapper there!"

"Oh, thanks. I'm headed to the hospital's holiday party and need a last-minute Secret Santa gift."

"Have something in mind, or do you want to browse?"

Greg checks his watch, saying, "Actually, I'm running late." He gives Vera a quick smile. "And I'd completely trust your choice?"

"Not feeling the Christmas spirit?" she asks while heading to a display on the side wall.

"Eh," he says with a shrug.

When she turns, holding a decorative white-string snowman with twig arms and a black top hat, she pauses with an eyebrow raised until Greg nods. "Want it wrapped?" Vera asks on her way to the checkout counter.

"If you don't mind. It'll save me the trouble."

So Vera rips a large piece of giftwrap from several rolls mounted on the wall. "Bringing a special lady to this party?" she asks over her shoulder.

And he sees it, the twinkle in her eye.

It's another reason he's sitting out this season of love—that hopeful look folks get at the thought of a holiday romance. Because *his* hopes have a track record of being brusquely dashed.

"No, no date this time. How about you?" It's a tactic that always works: Change the subject and the hopeful date-questions fade. "You and Derek? Everything good with you guys?"

"Yes, *when* we manage to see each other!" Vera says while taping the snowman box closed and folding giftwrap around it. "This is my busiest time of year, and he's getting things ready for his Deck the Boats Festival."

Greg wanders over to the window and pets Jingles, who is now sitting on the sill. "Derek puts on quite a show on the cove."

"He does."

Vera flips the box, creases the wrapping paper, tapes it up, then ties a wide ribbon around the gift. As she does, she gives Greg a concerned glance or two. When their eyes meet, he can't miss her subtle sad smile, as though she's sympathetic to his single status.

"Why don't you help yourself to one of my sister's doughnuts?" she asks, hitching her thumb to the baked goods case. "She makes them fresh, daily. And, well, it'll get you in the holiday spirit!"

Seriously? If this keeps up—drowning his sorrows in sugar—he'll be needing to add a few laps to his daily workout. For now, he walks to the glass-domed case and lifts out a pity doughnut. "What kind is it?"

"Chocolate-custard-filled." After ringing up his purchase, she puts the wrapped snowman in a big bag. "And here, take a napkin," she adds. "You'll be covered in sugar otherwise."

Walking outside to his car, Greg's got his wrapped gift in one hand, and the overloaded doughnut tucked in a napkin in the other. He glances at the blue waters of the cove, and at Vera's historical Dutch colonial beside her Christmas shop on the cove's banks. Strung white lights outline the house's widow's walk, setting it a-twinkling in the twilight.

As he takes in the holiday décor first, then considers the loaded doughnut in hand, a thought occurs to him. The *old* Greg Davis would've passed on the bulging pastry to save his appetite for the holiday party dinner—no doubt some stuffed chicken breast or filet mignon meal.

Well, walking toward his 1968 Mustang Fastback, the *new* Greg Davis throws caution to the wind. Yes, he does what the *old* Greg would *never* do—he takes a big bite of that sinful sweet in his hand, sinking his teeth right into the soft doughnut.

And … *bada boom!*

Like a geyser, doughnut filling spews from the other end of the pastry. An explosion of chocolate custard and white-powdered sugar erupts, landing—of course—across the front of his perfectly appropriate, nicely-coordinated-with-gray-pants, burgundy cashmere sweater.

❦

"Yoo-hoo!"

If Greg wasn't so busy smearing the chocolate custard even more, he'd look up at the woman's voice. Folding his paper napkin in half, he drags it across the brown smear on his once-very-fine sweater.

"Oh, *yoo-hoo!*" sounds out again, more insistently this time.

Insistently enough to get Greg to glance up in the direction of the woman's voice.

A familiar woman, at that. A woman with straight

blonde bangs peeking out from beneath her slouchy wool beanie. A woman leaning out the window of her SUV pulled curbside at the entranceway to the cove.

An SUV with a tiny house hitched behind it.

Greg steps closer when she waves him over. Steps closer, while again biting into that mammoth doughnut just to stem the dripping filling. He points to his sweater. "Just my luck," he calls out to Lindsey.

"It'll come out in the wash." She hands him a few more napkins through her driver's window. "Doesn't look *too* bad."

"It is, though," he says, still swiping at the creamy chocolate mess, "if you're on your way to the hospital's holiday party at the boathouse on the river." As he says it, he stuffs the last of the gooey doughnut into his mouth, then dabs at the custard on his sweater, which makes more of a splotch. "And now my outfit's ruined." He checks his watch, then gives one more pathetic pat to his sweater.

"Oh, no. You're on your way there? Right *now?* Well listen, I was just about to turn around here and head home. It's been a busy day at the Merry Market." She glances out toward the lapping cove up ahead. "But ... I have an idea."

Greg looks up from his smearing.

"You've come to the right place," Lindsey says before motioning for him to follow her and her hitched tiny house straight to the cove parking lot.

By the time Greg catches up with Lindsey, her SUV is parked, and her *Vagabond Vintage* sign is snapped open and set beside the steps to her doorway. She stands inside the golden shingled tiny house, just beyond the open door, and whisks him inside.

"Careful stepping around Santa!" Lindsey exclaims while pointing to her old-world Santa figure propped just inside the shop. "I think you met him the other day? During our fender bender?"

Greg walks in and looks around, all in a few seconds flat. That's how tiny the space is. From a small fold-down table between two padded benches; to a sink and counter area across from a couch; to a shelf of shoes and leather purses beneath a rack of clothes that Lindsey is brushing through, it takes no time to scan. Stepping further inside, he bends a little beneath the low ceiling.

"You actually have *everything* in here?" he asks. "I mean, for your shop?"

"I do. I have to be very self-contained for not only my life on the road, but to have my pop-up shop easily accessible, too."

Easily accessible? Greg thinks he can reach out and touch just about everything from where he stands. As a matter of fact, he tests this accessibility theory. First, a discreet touch to the old-school turntable set up on a side shelf. Next? He skims a framed map hanging over the kitchenette table. When he turns, Lindsey is holding a brown leather vest and button-down shirt.

"Lucky you, I can open up shop for emergency

situations like yours." She raises the two hangers higher. "Will these work?"

"Work?"

"Sure. Because you can't wear that to your party." While stepping closer, she nods to Greg's sloppy sweater.

"I guess it could," Greg decides while taking the two items, then looking beyond Lindsey. "Do you have a dressing room?"

"Over here." She points to the far end of her tiny house, where a floor-to-ceiling curtain hangs on a rod in front of a very small room. "When this *isn't* my store, the dressing room is a powder room. You'll have space to change in there." As she explains, she walks down the short hall and slides open the heavy curtain.

Okay, so maybe this doughnut fiasco was supposed to happen, in the scheme of things. Maybe it's actually a part of his metamorphosis. Because when Greg looks in the mirror after putting on the leather vest, there's a distinct transformation. Even the shirt he tried on works.

It can't be missed in his reflection. The change is eye-opening.

He'd been dressed wrong, all wrong. And it's time for a makeover. No—a *man-over*!

Because a cashmere cardigan actually suited the *old* Greg Davis. The one who drove a luxury sedan, of course.

But a vintage brown leather vest, one creased and worn in all the right places? Over this checked button-down? Definitely suited to the new Greg Davis he's been testing out lately. "Not bad. Not bad at all," he whispers before opening the dressing room curtain. "This'll do," he calls to Lindsey.

Lindsey hurries over and tugs at the side of the vest. "Wait." She steps back and squints at his ensemble. "You need a tie!" She picks one from a small selection, saying, "Fashion is all about details, including the finishing touch."

When she turns around holding a dark tie, Greg takes it and puts it on, tucking it behind the deep V of the leather vest.

"Okay." Lindsey stands, crooked finger to her chin. "Walk down the hall so I can check the fit." She nods toward her fold-down table at the far end of her house.

Greg hesitates, first looking down at his new threads, then walking past her so that she can see the back of his vest, too. But when he gets to her table, he's so intrigued by that framed map covered with pushpins, he stops right in front of it.

"What's with all the pins?" Greg asks.

Standing beside him now, Lindsey explains. "This is my corkboard map. And the pushpins mark either the places I've been, or the places I want to go to set up my shop. Where you see a red," she says while pointing out some red pins, "I've visited. Greens are my dream stops." Standing close, she glances up at him. "I've always been a bit of a dreamer."

Greg can see that. In the uncomfortable pause that falls between them in this tiny house-on-wheels; in the record turntable stacked with old albums; in the racks of vintage clothing, everything about Lindsey Haynes points to a fancy-free, bohemian life.

Behind him, Lindsey takes a sharp breath and gives a clap of her hands. "Okay, then." She squeezes past and quickly closes up shop, starting with securing her rack of clothes.

"What do I owe you for the vest and shirt?" Greg asks.

"After backing my house into you, those items are, well, they're *on* the house."

"No, that's not necessary."

"Really, I'm happy to help, Greg," she tells him over her shoulder. "So, are you feeling the groove?" she asks then, motioning to his rockin' leather vest.

Before he can answer, she's rushing down the few steps outside her door and snapping shut her *Vagabond Vintage* sign. "Ready to mingle and jingle at that holiday party?" she asks, breezing back inside. "And dance with your date?"

"Date? Well, no. But ... Thank you, but there's no date tonight."

"Aww." Lindsey sets her folded-up sign behind one of the benches. "She couldn't make it?"

He's not sure why, but suddenly Greg feels trapped. Complaining about holiday heartbreak to his brother, or father, is one thing. But to this inquisitive woman standing there with a slouchy beanie on her head and an expectant look in her eyes, eyes brushed by long wisps of blonde bangs, yes, he feels ... confined. Like he can't escape her look, or her judgment.

"Haven't had a steady girl in three years, actually," he admits. "So I know what I'm in for." Greg glances out the window toward the cove. The low-setting sun casts a dull light on the dark water. "Walking into that boathouse solo? Let's just say it'll be an uncomfortable ordeal." Now, well now that he said it, he looks at her and shrugs.

"What do you mean?"

"Lots of prying questions headed my way. *You seeing somebody, Doc? Would you like my sister's number?* You get the idea."

Lindsey nods.

"Friendly-enough folks, my coworkers," Greg continues. "But I'll just be glad when the party's over. Because it all turns into an embarrassing fix-up event of sorts when you walk in alone."

Lindsey moves to tuck her old-world Santa into a secure corner, then turns and eyes Greg. "Well … I *am* closing up shop for the day. And after hitting your car, I certainly wouldn't mind making amends."

"Amends? How so? Because these clothes are more than enough."

Lindsey Haynes does it then.

Yes, she saves him from a night of awkward fix-ups, of possible pairings. It all happens when she tips her head and turns up her hands. "Still. I could always go *with* you to your party, Dr. Davis," she offers. "I mean, you know, as a favor. Just to deflect the single crowd."

nine

IF THERE'S ONE THING GREG hasn't tired of, it's sitting in the driver's seat of his '68 Mustang. Like he's doing now, parked outside Lindsey's tiny house after she towed it back to Snowflake Lake. While waiting for her to change into a formal outfit for the hospital party, he cranks open his window a bit, then sits back and takes in the lakeside view. White lights twinkle on the community Christmas tree. The little cabins are decorated, too. They're framed in colorful lights; garland loops across porch railings; golden lamplight spills from paned windows.

Suddenly, a familiar noise approaches. A *putt-putt-puttering* ...

"That you, Dr. Davis?" Gus asks from his snowtorcycle as he pulls alongside Greg's car. "Thought I recognized those spiffy wheels. Any regrets yet? How's she handling the snowy roads?"

"Not bad," Greg answers while cranking his window all the way open. "A little slip-sliding. That'll stop once I get some good snow tires."

Gus leans over and peers inside Greg's dark car. "So. What brings you around these parts this evening? My arm's much better and doesn't really need a checkup."

"No, I'm not here for that tonight." Greg adjusts his rearview mirror before continuing. "It's more for a holiday work-party thing. Lindsey's, well … umm … coming along."

"Oh, a date, then?"

"No! No, not a date. It's not like that." Greg bends and glances out through the windshield toward Lindsey's tiny house. "Your niece is just doing me a favor, and … well … it's kind of complicated, Gus."

At that moment, the tiny house's front door opens and Lindsey steps outside dressed in a faux-fur jacket over a fitted black velvet dress. As she hurries down the steps, Greg looks from Gus, to Lindsey, then back to Gus—just in time to see him tip up his tweed cap and raise an eyebrow at Greg. After a gloved wave, Gus gives his snowtorcycle a rev and putters off toward his cabin on this cold December night.

❧

It's clearly obvious to Lindsey that no one does Christmas like the Addison Boathouse. The two-story building with a massive deck is all a-twinkling in white lights. Wreaths hang on every door; spotlights shine on riverside trees. Why, walking with Greg up the stairs to the entrance has her feeling a bit like Cinderella!

After leaving their coats at the coat-check counter, Lindsey turns to see more of the same grandeur in the ballroom. A tall Christmas tree towers in the center of the dance floor. Swags of garland sweep overhead. There is food, and a jazz band, and happy people everywhere. Happy people who, when they spot Greg Davis, veer close.

"Dr. Davis?" the first woman asks, her eyes shifting from Greg to Lindsey. "Introductions are in order."

"Who's *this* lovely lady?" another woman inquires.

"You've been keeping a secret!" a man remarks as he clasps Greg's shoulder.

"Greg! Where've you been hiding your … friend?" another asks while dancing past with a sequin-dressed woman in his arms.

Just like he knew they would, the curious questions begin. It's no wonder Greg was reluctant to show up at this party.

And that reluctance shows in the way Greg stammers, and in the way he's clenching his jaw. Inquisitive coworkers and acquaintances ask him who he's with, stressing him enough that he fumbles through the first few introductions.

"Well," he says while looking at Lindsey beside him, "this is my, well …"

"Hi!" Because enough is enough. It's time to take over in the hospital's holiday-party-inquiry department. After all, wasn't her purpose here to deflect the single crowd?

"I'm Greg's girlfriend, Lindsey. Lindsey Haynes. I own a vintage clothing boutique," she says to one woman. "Maybe you've seen it in the Merry Market?" to another.

The questions keep coming, though.

Weren't you in the local paper?
Didn't you hit your boyfriend's car?

"I did!" Lindsey assures their tipped heads, their raised eyebrows. "But luckily Greg doesn't hold that against me. Isn't that right, honey?" she asks with a flirty wink tossed Greg's way.

Walking to their table, the questions continue. Until, finally, a familiar voice calls out their names.

"Greg! Over here!"

They both turn to see Frank Lombardo standing with his arms crossed over his chest. He's practically in shadow at the side wall.

"Frank," Greg says as they hurry over. But Lindsey feels it, then, how he slows his step and glances at her beside him. "Frank," he says again. "I'd like you to meet Lindsey."

"Heck, Lindsey and I are old friends." Frank warmly shakes her hand. "She wrangled me into a photo shoot, chopping wood out at the lake."

"And the hat and scarf you modeled sold right away!" Lindsey tells him.

"Good to know. And hey, nice to see you both here." Frank motions between the two of them. "Together?"

Lindsey does it. Because it doesn't matter if it's one of

91

Greg's friends, or merely work acquaintances. Yes, she plays the girlfriend role to a T, nodding as she loops her arm through Greg's and leans into him. "Look, they're starting the sing-along. I'd love to join in," she says, trying to extricate Greg from his friend's prying question, his smiling eyes, his waiting-for-an-answer patience.

"Okay," Greg says as they turn toward the DJ at the far end of the room.

"Yo, Doc," Frank calls after them. "You game for a practice run tomorrow?"

"Run?" Lindsey asks.

"Yeah," Frank explains. "Your boyfriend needs to *practice* for the Santa's Run 5K."

"You're on, Lombardo. What time?" Greg asks.

Frank checks his schedule on his phone. "I have some teddy-bear tea party gig in the morning. Something my sister, Gina, holds for the kids here."

"Okay, and I'm having snow tires put on the 'stang first thing. So we'll meet up after a quick lunch?" Greg asks as he leads Lindsey toward the crowd singing and swaying around the room's grand Christmas tree.

"If you can keep up with me," Frank calls through the warbling crowd.

Greg turns and while walking backward, calls back, "You're going down, man!"

By that time, they're in the thick of it. The thick of holly, jolly Christmas carols—right as the sing-along begins. Lindsey and Greg harmonize about decking the halls, and taking sleigh rides. Afterward, they enjoy their dinner, have drinks, chat with Greg's colleagues.

And Lindsey never lets up. A promise is a promise, after all.

So she continues playing the girlfriend part, through and through. As the curious questions fly Greg's way—innocent raised-eyebrow questions asking about his date—oh, Lindsey lays it on thick. Her fingers stroke Greg's arm; she tugs his tie and ruffles his hair; tells people about her Vagabond Vintage shop while leaning close to Greg; kisses his cheek under the mistletoe. Anything it takes to keep any fix-ups at bay.

Until finally, Greg whispers in her ear. "Let's dance. At least we'll be safe from curious coworkers on the dance floor."

Maybe. Or … maybe not.

༄

As Greg walks to the dance floor, he tugs his distressed leather vest, cuffs his shirtsleeves and gets ready for some jolly jiving. His coworkers are boppin' and swinging, swaying and shuffling—utterly feeling the holiday spirit.

"Dr. *Davis*," Lindsey says as he unleashes some fancy footwork while holding her in his arms. "I never thought you'd be so sure on your feet!"

As he half spins her, getting her black velvet dress twirling against her legs, Greg tells her, "I ruled the ballroom domain in high school. Won the dance-off trophy two years running."

The more they dip and foot-stomp, boogie and bend, something happens, though.

Something Greg never saw coming.

Women want to cut in and dance with this *new* Greg Davis. Snag a dance with the doctor sporting an unexpected look in his fitted leather vest and unshaven face. The ladies keep interrupting his dances with Lindsey.

The thing is, the old Greg Davis would've obliged them. He would've been fair and given everyone a twirl around the floor.

But the new Greg Davis? Oh, no. The new Greg Davis shrugs them off and simply spins Lindsey away, leaving surprised expressions on each and every woman's face.

But still, with each look of dismay, he hears something—phrases that have his heart sinking. The disappointed words ring out over the jolly jingles of the cranking Christmas tunes:

> *Maybe Friday, Dr. Davis! I'll see you there with my paddle …*
> *Bringing a hefty checkbook to that one …*
> *I'm claiming you Friday, there's no escaping me there …*

Greg notices something else, too, no matter how often he spins Lindsey away from the women wanting to cut in on their dance. Yes, he sees how Lindsey takes this all in like she's at a Ping-Pong tournament, her head turning this way and that. That's how often they're interrupted.

Elderly women, young, tall, short … doesn't matter. The interruptions keep coming.

I like that leather vest! You wear it when I cash in next week.

"Cash in?" Lindsey asks with a glance past Greg's shoulder to a woman waggling a finger at him as she says it.

"It's just another event I'm obligated to attend." Greg joins her glance at the woman behind him, still waggling. "A really hokey holiday thing I got roped into. Even though it's for a good cause, I'm ashamed to admit that it actually borders on embarrassing." He dances Lindsey across the floor, away from that waggling woman. "So I'm dreading that night in particular."

"Dreading?" She turns and gives the woman another doubtful look. "How bad can it be?"

Oh, if she only knew.

The word Greg wanted to use wasn't even *embarrassing*. It was more like … *humiliating*. But there's no way out of his charitable commitment; he'll show up like always and get it over with.

Obviously to much delight—apparent in the women's sing-song voices now …

Oh, Greg! Only a few more days until the paddles will be flipping.
After next week, you'll be mine, all mine.
Friday is fun-day.

The only way to escape it, to distract Lindsey from the merry mania, is to dip her, then twirl her away from the smiling women as the dance goes on.

⁓

Just like that? It happens. The party is over.

Greg got through it with Lindsey on his arm. She saved him, actually. Saved him from any awkward set-ups and dead-end blind dates. From any flirting and hopeful looks. So if that's what came from her tiny house hitting his car, tonight it all feels worth it.

Walking out of the boathouse with Lindsey still playing the girlfriend gig and looping her arm through his, a thought occurs to Greg. As Lindsey chatters about the fun festivities, and the delicious meal, and the nice people, Greg can't help but ponder this one thought.

All the way through the parking lot, as they wave goodbye to other guests leaving, as he opens the Mustang's passenger door and Lindsey gets inside—wrapping her faux-fur coat tight around her in the chilly night air—he knows his thought is true.

Yes, the old Greg Davis would've asked Lindsey Haynes for a nightcap at Cedar Ridge Tavern. Or the old Greg Davis would've taken her for a stroll along Main Street, then for a spin on the Holly Trolley.

But. But, but, *but*.

The new Greg Davis is a new man and doesn't. Doesn't suggest a late-evening coffee, or a hand-in-hand walk. Doesn't ask to see her again. Sticking to his Christmas commitment to keep his heart intact, there will be none of that. Instead he drops her off at her tiny house with only a nod of thanks.

So when he gets home to his condominium, he's surprised to receive a text message from Lindsey.

Now that wasn't so bad, was it? she asks.

Good question.

Greg hangs up his long black wool coat, puts away his leather gloves, turns on a shelf stereo in his living room, then walks to the front paned window.

"*Lindsey Haynes*," he whispers while shaking his head. Outside, candles flicker in the neighboring colonials' windows; a glittery Santa waves from beside a lamppost in a front yard; two birch deer stand on stick legs on a nearby bungalow's porch.

Looking out on the cold, dark night, Greg lingers there while his foot taps to the beat of a Christmas carol playing behind him in the living room.

ten

LINDSEY HAYNES THOUGHT SHE'D SEEN it all.

That is, until Sunday morning, when she arrives with her new friend Penny at Addison's annual Christmas trunk sale on the covered bridge. During the holiday event, the bridge is closed to any vehicles and traffic is rerouted.

As they approach the covered bridge, light snow falling makes the scene look straight off a holiday card penned with festive greetings. Further inside the bridge, trunks of every size, shape and color await—tops open, goods spilling out. This busy trunk sale is a neighborhood affair, and families have brought old steamer trunks; packing trunks; footlockers; blanket chests; humpbacks and doll trunks. Old and new; vinyl, leather and wood. Better yet, each and every trunk holds some sort of Christmas treasure: ornaments, décor, unique gift items.

But it's the banner strung across the entrance that Lindsey's never before seen the likes of: *Lots o' junque in our trunks!*

"*Christmas* junk," Penny explains as they near. "It's like a holiday flea market, where folks swap, bargain and sell real one-of-a-kind finds. There's something for everyone."

"Well now. This is just what I need to replenish my Vagabond Vintage inventory," Lindsey tells her as she's already eyeing a trunk of fur muffs. She picks up a white one, slips in her hands and raises the soft, furry muff to her cheek. "Definitely buying one of these," she admits.

While Lindsey pays for the muff, Penny moves to the next trunk in line. "I need a decoration for my desk at Suitcase Escapes." She turns back to Lindsey. "That's the travel agency where I work," she says while lifting a lacy tabletop angel, then setting it back down.

But a trunk across from Penny gets Lindsey's attention, and she veers in that direction, all while listening to Penny chat.

"Frank tells me he saw you last night at the hospital's holiday party? At the boathouse?" Penny asks.

"Yes! Wow, he put on quite a gala. There was caroling, and Christmas games, an amazing dinner. And then dancing beneath the twinkling lights." Lindsey lifts a woman's plaid coat from a large steamer trunk. "It was really a magical night," she says over her shoulder to Penny.

"Hmm, magical? Frank says you were there with Greg." Penny stops at a blanket chest beside the clothing steamer trunk Lindsey is still brushing through. "Greg Davis?"

Oh, Lindsey hears it—that flirty lilt to Penny's words. And Lindsey's quick to squash any romantic insinuations. "I *was*, actually," she says while running her fingers along the seam of a polka-dot minidress now, then turning to a woman sitting on a stool beside the antique trunk. "Is this from the sixties?"

The woman nods. "It was my aunt's. I have a photograph of her wearing it in 1967."

"Far out!" Lindsey considers the dress, then folds it back into the trunk. "I'm still looking around, though." She catches up to Penny two trunks down and leans close. "Like I said, I *was* with Greg last night. But I was doing him a favor, that's all," she adds with a small smile.

"But Frank said you were introduced as Greg's girlfriend! And I'm so thrilled for Greg. He deserves a nice girl like you," Penny continues as she sets down a pinecone snowman and moseys on to the next trunk with Lindsey. "What a happy accident, bumping into him the way you did, Linz."

"No, no." Lindsey spots a hint of leather beneath the pile of clothes in the trunk, so she digs in for that piece. "We're not together. Not like that … well, not at all." Her hand finds the leather article and pulls it up from beneath sweaters and dresses. "Long story short, Penny? On his way to the party, Greg spilled something on his shirt and I was close by, with my shop?"

Penny tips her head, squinting while listening as if she's not fully believing this seemingly convoluted story—even though it's not.

"So he needed a new outfit, plus an exit strategy for the party." Lindsey pulls out a black leather bomber from the old trunk. "And I fit the bill," she adds with a shrug.

"So you're *not* dating?"

Lindsey shakes her head with another small smile, then raises the jacket higher.

"But … maybe he'll call you?" Penny asks.

"No. It really wasn't like that. Greg made a mess with a *doughnut*, believe it or not, and needed a new shirt. I had one in my shop, and really? Going with him to the party was a one-time thing to get him through an awkward night."

"Aw, too bad." Penny walks to a black trunk with gold straps. There she lifts out a tabletop ceramic Christmas tree. "You'd be so cute together."

Lindsey turns the men's leather bomber over in her hands, feeling the worn leather, checking the pockets, tugging the zipper. The jacket seems straight out of the 1970s, and would make a nice gift idea on her shop's website. "Anyway, Penny. It's for the best that I don't get entangled with Greg—or with *anyone* right now. Because I'm really just passing through Addison and will be on the road again soon."

As she says the words to her friend whose hopeful smile has turned sad, what Lindsey doesn't count on is this: the surprising way her *own* smile fades, too.

"Glad you could come along on your day off, Dad," Greg says to Pete beside him. The two men stand in front of a wall of tires at the local automotive shop. The smell of new rubber permeates the showroom, and ceiling spotlights shine on the week's specials. Beneath each tire is a placard noting the qualities of each. "What do you think? Studded or not?" Greg asks.

"Not sure." Pete reaches up and runs his hand across a studded tire. "Son," he says, "this is so unlike you. Going through all this rigmarole when you can just get your old car back from Dave's Auto Body. I'm sure he'd work with you to swap it for the Mustang."

Greg turns to face his father directly. Pete has a scarf looped around his neck beneath a flannel-lined jacket. "Dad," Greg says. "This is the *new* Greg Davis now, who drives a fully refurbished 1968 Mustang Fastback." With that, he extends his hand to his father's for a shake.

Pete obliges, but reluctantly. "And I'm not sure I like this new Greg Davis."

"Why not?" Greg motions to the *Good, Better, Best* tire display nearby. "I'm being safe and reliable, like you've always said. Look. I'm even equipping my sports car with the very best winter tires." He walks to a floor display. "Now I just have to decide on all-season, performance or purely snow tires."

When a salesman walks over, Greg deliberates the merits of the three tire types, and of studded versus studless.

"You'll get anywhere from five-to-twenty percent

improved performance with the snow tires. Today's winter tires really deliver," the salesman explains. "The traction is unmatched, even *without* studs—which are pretty noisy on dry pavement."

Greg hesitates, unsure if he wants any sound competing with his 'stang's rumbling engine.

"Son? You can always toss a couple bags of sand in your trunk to help maneuver in the snow," Pete adds.

"And go with four snow tires instead of two, to get optimum control in any conditions," the salesman advises.

So after choosing the best of the studless tires, Greg and his father head to the customer waiting area. Old magazines are stacked on a small table; the overhead TV is tuned to a sports channel; the vending machine is filled with cheap pastries in plastic packages.

Greg takes off his long wool coat and hangs it on a wall hook. When he looks through a large window into the service bays, he sees his Mustang up on the lift already. The technician is removing one of the car's current tires.

"What's that you're wearing?" Pete asks him.

Greg lifts the hem of his leather vest and turns to where his father is sitting. "This? A vest, Dad."

"But it's ... leather. Where's your sweater vest?"

"No, Dad," Greg insists as he sits in a padded folding chair beside his father. "Sweater vest was the *old* Greg Davis. Get it?"

"Watch it, son, because you're sounding mercurial now."

"*Mercurial?*" Greg repeats. "Jeez, Dad. What did you do, find that in your handy-dandy pocket thesaurus?"

"Mercurial, impulsive. I just don't get it … this new person you're becoming. So, you going out somewhere today with that snazzy vest? Some dinner or something?"

"Wore it last night, actually. At the hospital's holiday party over at the boathouse. They put on a nice shindig this year."

"Really. And how'd it go? Good food? Big crowd?"

"Very swanky," Greg says as he walks to the vending machine, inserts a dollar and makes his choice. "Great dinner, caroling, music and dancing." He bends and lifts out his package of miniature cinnamon-topped coffee cakes. "Want one?" he asks while ripping open the wrapping.

"Sure." Pete takes a coffee cake and bites in. "You meet anybody last night?" he asks around the pastry. "So I can start hoping for a grandbuck?"

Greg sits again, his hand holding the other coffee cake. "You keep saying that, Dad, and we'll have to stop hanging out like this." With that, he stuffs half the cake into his mouth. "*Grandbuck*," he whispers, shaking his head.

"Okay, fine. But an old man can dream, can't he?"

Ah, dreams, Greg thinks. Look where they got him. Because he's had plenty of holiday dreams the past few years. Dreams of finding the right special someone to spend Christmas with … maybe New Year's Eve, too. That's all. Someone to make the holidays sweet.

Dreams that evaporated like a winter mist.

"Well, for your information, I didn't meet anyone.

Believe me," Greg says, finishing the last of his coffee cake, "the *old* Greg Davis would've tried. But this is the *new* Greg Davis." He stands, walks to the service-bay observation window, then turns back to his father. "So I *went* with someone instead. But just as friends. It took off all that pressure to line up a holiday date, which I'm passing on this year. I brought that Lindsey."

"The one who *hit* you with her tiny house? You're *seeing* each other now?"

"No!" Greg looks again as the technician spins lug nuts onto his new deep-treaded snow tires out in the shop. After a second, Greg paces the room, then explains things. "No, Dad. Lindsey did me a favor. Said she wanted to make amends for hitting my car. So she came along just so I wouldn't have to hear the women there trying to fix me up. Or wrangle a pity date out of me— which would get me nothing but a first date."

"What's wrong with a first date?"

"I'll tell you what. They never lead to a second date for me. And I'm sick of being a first-date man, okay?" Greg sits again, this time picking up a magazine, turning it over, then setting it back on the table. "So believe me, Lindsey being there kept the night easy, for once. But that's all it was. And she's leaving town soon, anyway. Lindsey is. She's one of those free-spirit types."

"Yup. Free to stay, too."

"You have to stop jumping to conclusions, Dad. We had one fake date, that's all. *Fake*—to throw people off. It was nothing."

Problem is, Greg's been telling himself that a few too many times, as though he has to convince himself. He thinks now of how Lindsey jumped right in and introduced herself last night as his girlfriend. She came through for him, just to avoid awkward situations. She rubbed his arm, kissed his cheek, danced close. Laughed.

"Davis?" a clerk calls from the checkout counter. "Greg Davis?"

Greg stands, motioning his hand.

"You're all set," the clerk says, holding up Greg's keys and the snow-tire paperwork. "Nice and safe now. With that heavy-duty tread on those tires, there'll be no spinouts for you."

Greg pays, takes his keys and drops them in the pocket of his leather vest, then slips on his black wool coat.

And the whole time, what he knows is this: *Some* spinouts are unavoidable, like spinouts of the heart.

Because, wait ... What's this? With thoughts of Lindsey dancing in his arms last night, beneath sparkling Christmas lights, he's already starting to feel something— uh-oh, it's his own heart beginning to slip-slide. And it makes him want to slam on the brakes, this emotional spinout does.

Slam on the brakes to romance, keep a safe distance from one particular female acquaintance, and continue on in his single, confirmed-bachelor way.

eleven

MOST PEOPLE USE ALARM CLOCKS. Most people are jolted from sleep by the loud music of that alarm, or a blaring beep sound, or a jangling bell.

Not Lindsey Haynes. No, Lindsey wakes up to her coffeemaker.

That's right. Each night, she sets the automatic timer on her coffeemaker, and each morning she wakes up to a sweet aroma of fresh-brewed coffee. Instead of jangling, jarring alarms, she listens to the bubbling sound of percolating java. It allows her to snuggle beneath the blankets in her bed, beneath the peaked ceiling in the tiny house loft, as the aroma wafts through her home.

But Tuesday morning, her ringing cell phone beats the coffeemaker—and now she's talking while nestled beneath the blankets, all as the scent of coffee starts to rise.

"Oh, Mom. Uncle Gus is so nice. I had dinner with him, and he leaves cute care baskets on my doorstep. You know, little treats, like something to snack on, or a holiday book. Yesterday, he left me a pair of fuzzy socks."

"I'm glad someone's there to check in with you, Lindsey. It's nice to be close to family. But Dad and I are wondering if we'll see you for Christmas?"

"Of course! The Merry Market's been great, here in Addison. It's bringing in lots of customers and keeping me so busy, I haven't even thought ahead to the holiday." Lindsey sits up, inhales the fresh coffee aroma and glances out the paned loft window toward Snowflake Lake. The wild grasses surrounding it are coated with white frost, looking like tatted lace. "For now, I'm going to stay on a little longer anyway. But don't worry, I'll be home for Christmas."

"Okay, hon. At least Uncle Gus will be around in the meantime. So I won't worry *too* much. You let me know if you need anything."

"I will." With the coffee proving too much a temptation, Lindsey heads to her loft stairs. "Talk to you soon, Mom. And say hi to Dad for me. Love you!"

Going downstairs in her pajamas and slippers, Lindsey thinks this is her new favorite time of day: pouring her coffee, then checking for a daily care package from Gus. Sure enough, there's a basket on her step again today. She brings it inside to her tiny table, sips her steaming coffee and unpacks the basket.

"Breakfast is served," she whispers upon finding a wrapped slice of coffee cake, a container of raspberries, and, okay, birdseed for the feeder outside, along with the latest edition of the *Addison Weekly*.

After arranging her cake and fruit on a plate, she stops only to put a scratchy old Christmas album on her record player, then turns back to her food while opening the paper. As Sinatra sings about those jing-jingle bells, Lindsey taps her foot and finds the paper's *Weekly Wondering* feature. In it, the Roving Reporter asks residents timely questions that are all the buzz in town. This week he asks for opinions about the new traffic roundabout.

"Oh, now *this* should be good!" Lindsey leans closer as she takes a bite of the coffee cake and reads on.

From Lillian March, Adult-Ed Art Teacher: "The roundabout is just okay. But you must be very careful and watch for pedestrians! And it's a little too small, making it hard to cut turns."

From Tyler, clerk at Cooper Hardware: "That roundabout's sick, man. You can get in and out real fast. Thumbs-up, dude."

From Mrs. Crenshaw, retired: "I don't like it. Not one bit. It's one big mess! All those hesitant drivers stopping in the middle of it, almost causing accidents. It's very dangerous, and the traffic is not smooth."

Lindsey deliberates on the three opinions and decides that she agrees most with Lillian March. When she turns the page, there's a guest article from meteorologist Leo Sterling. "Hmm," she says, carefully reading his weather lore. *My canine assistant, Captain, has determined—through his unusually thick coat of fur—that many more flurries will be falling. So keep your eyes to the skies!*

Oh, please! Lindsey thinks. The last time she did *that*, a mini-minor catastrophe ensued with a certain gruff doctor in this quirky little town. So she quickly turns the page to find something more calming to her blood pressure. "Ah, yes. *Holiday Happenings*. Maybe there's something here I can do to get into the Christmas spirit." She scoops up a few raspberries, pops them in her mouth and leans close to the paper again. Some of the events listed are familiar to her, like the ongoing Merry Market on The Green. There's been a lot of chatter there, too, about this Deck the Boats Festival—a grand boat parade on Addison Cove, all in memory of a local little girl who lost her life there years ago now.

Then … Lindsey pulls the paper closer. "What's this?" she asks. "A Christmas Auction at The Historical Society?" If any holiday event is right up her alley, this would be it. Maybe she can attend and bid on something for Vagabond Vintage. So she sips her coffee and reads the sampling of donated items going up for auction: Circa 1765 Antiques donated a tambour mantel clock; Snowflakes and Coffee Cakes Christmas Shoppe donated an assortment of blown-glass teardrop ornaments; Wedding Wishes bridal boutique donated a lacy 1960s wedding gown.

"Perfect," Lindsey says, drawing her finger beneath the Wedding Wishes listing. There are so many Christmastime wedding proposals, her customers would certainly like a chance to buy a vintage wedding gown of ivory satin and lace. Yes … with its straight skirt, pillbox hat with netting, buttons up the back and detachable train, it would sell in no time. Actually, the more she looks at the picture of the dress, the more Lindsey wants it. Already planning how she'll photograph it for her website, well, she just can't stop thinking about it.

Until …

Until she reads the next item up for bid:

Back by popular demand. Our most coveted item is on the auction block again this year. For the past three years running, this item has outbid all others! Yes, Addison's most eligible bachelor returns. Get your paddles ready, ladies … for a date with Dr. Greg Davis!

Those three words—Dr. Greg Davis—get Lindsey sputtering on her coffee as she looks at the photograph of Greg. It's a recent snapshot taken outdoors, maybe at the cove in the fall. Standing casually near the water, he wears a canvas jacket over a flannel shirt. His light brown hair is mussed in a breeze; his smile easy; his blue eyes squinting in the sun. So this is the event he said was too embarrassing to even talk about.

He's an auctioned date!

Now she gets it.

That's what the women at the hospital's holiday party were referring to with their mentions of *Maybe Friday!* And *I'll see you there with my paddle.* And *Bringing a hefty checkbook to that one … You'll be mine, all mine, come Friday.*

"Golly gumdrops!" Lindsey whispers. "Bidding for a *date?*"

Sitting at her table, she reads the write-up once more, then gazes out the window toward Snowflake Lake—

111

where a low mist hovers over the water.

That's what all the fuss was about.

∽◦

After a busy morning at the medical complex, Greg's surprised to be meeting Wes for lunch at Addison's dog park, especially in this cold December air. But that's what Wes' voicemail directed—to grab some sandwiches from The Main Course and meet him at the entrance to the dog park. So Greg added a scarf beneath his black wool coat, got the food and now peels into the parking lot right on time.

When he spots Wes waiting with his German shepherd, Comet, Greg calls out to his brother. "Yo, Wesley! The Main Course was nice and warm with empty tables we could sit at. Good music playing on the sound system. Why are we eating here, outside where it's freezing?" he asks. "Just to walk your dog?"

Before Wes can even answer, many voices further in the park call out in unison, "*Woof! Woof!*" Greg glances beyond the doggie obstacle course, then follows Wes to an empty nearby bench, its wooden backrest shaped like a giant dog biscuit. His brother's dressed in full post office uniform, right down to the blue hat with furry earflaps and blue parka, too—both with the appropriate USPS eagle insignia patch, front and center.

"No dog walks today, Scrubs," Wes says over his shoulder. "We're here to see Dad."

"Dad?" Greg hands Wes a paper-wrapped roast beef with horseradish on a hard roll. "Where is he?"

Wes hitches his head toward a Santa Claus sitting on another bench with a miniature dachshund beside him. That bench is draped with balsam garland, and mini wreaths hang from either end. "Look closely," Wes says.

Greg sets down a tray of two take-out sodas. He squints at a long line of people standing with leashed dogs before his gaze shifts to Santa.

Wait.

To his *father*, dressed as the jolly fella and patting the small dog beside him on the bench. Right then—on cue from a photographer—the crowd chants, "*Woof! Woof!*" precisely as the picture is snapped.

"Are you kidding me?" Greg asks while unwrapping his ham-and-Swiss. He lays the paper wrapping flat on his lap and lifts the stuffed sesame-seed roll.

"No." Wes bites into his own sandwich while holding Comet close on the leash.

"Dr. Davis!" a woman bundled in a fur-trimmed parka interrupts when she walks past with a yellow lab. "So good to see you."

Greg, nodding and chewing, thinks that the *old* Greg Davis would've taken his napkin, wiped his fingers and shook hands with her—a woman he recognizes from the medical building where he works. The *new* Greg Davis simply hitches his head and digs in for another bite of his lunch.

"So anyway." Wes lifts the roll of his half-eaten

sandwich, plucks out a small piece of the roast beef, then tosses it to Comet. "Dad and old man Cooper—"

"Derek?"

"No, Derek's *father*. This year, he and Dad have been competing for every Santa gig in town. The tree-lighting ceremony—which Cooper has all sewn up. The Sycamore Square Carol Sing, a church bazaar, Merry Market and … this. *Pawfect* Pics with Saint Nick."

Greg stuffs in another mouthful of his ham sandwich. "I've seen it all now," he says around the food. "Dad as Santa Claus—to the dogs."

"Yeah, I wanted to see this with my own eyes, too. Which is why I asked you to meet me *here* on your lunch hour." Wes opens a snack-sized bag of chips. "Plus I need you to squeeze Comet's cluck-cluck chicken toy. You know, to get his attention as the picture is snapped. Gets his ears up nice and straight." As he says it, Wes gives the rubbery chicken a squeak.

"For what? I mean, come on. You're really here to take a picture of *Comet* with Santa?"

"Absolutely. I need a new header pic for my social media."

"Dr. Davis?" another woman interrupts, approaching with her beagle on a leash. A snowflake-patterned cap is pulled over the woman's long brown hair, and she wears a wool jacket with toggle buttons. Greg recognizes her as a former patient of his. She stops beside him, eyeing him closely as he looks up at her from his bench seat. "I almost didn't recognize you beneath those … whiskers!"

Her gloved fingers lightly sweep across his cheek before she breezes off toward the doggie balance beam, all while managing another glance over her shoulder at Greg.

"Whiskers." Chewing a mouthful of potato chips, Wes looks closely at Greg. "You're not shaving now?"

"*Woof! Woof!*" resounds from the crowd then.

"Just today I didn't shave, for crying out loud," Greg answers his brother while turning up his collar against a cold wind. "Is there a law against that?" he asks, then sucks on his straw to slurp a swallow of soda.

"What's the matter with you lately?" Wes stuffs the last of his roast-beef-on-a-hard-roll into his mouth. "You're a town doctor and upstanding citizen. Need to look the part, bro."

Greg nods to Wes' face. "*You* don't shave. When's the last time a razor saw that mug of yours?"

"That's different. I'm a mailman."

"What's that supposed to mean? You represent the United States government!"

Suddenly a fluffy labradoodle veers close and tangles around the bench and Greg's legs. "Oh, watch out!" the woman holding the dog's leash exclaims. She squeezes around Greg in an attempt to untangle her dog. "Don't move." Carefully, she bends lower and slips the leash around Greg's legs, two times, just to unwrap it. As she straightens, she starts to apologize and walk away, but stops and gives Greg a double take. "Well, hi there! I'm Cassie." She extends her mittened hand to Greg's and shakes it. "And this is my dog, Lassie." Whether her cheeks are rosy from the cold air, or from being flustered, Greg can't tell. She glances to the Santa line. "Looks like you're next."

"Ladies first." Wes motions for her to get in front of them. "You go ahead."

"Why, thank you!" She tugs on her prancing Lassie's leash and gets in line.

Greg, shaking his head, finishes his sandwich. In a moment, he feels his brother nudging him. "What?" Greg asks.

"She's not so bad." Wes leans closer and lowers his voice. "Talk to her. Maybe you can wrangle a date out of this canine photo op."

"Seriously?" Greg checks out the woman. She wears a puffy vest over a thick sweater and skinny jeans. Her hat and gloves are a matched, cable-knit set. "She *rhymed* her dog's name to her own. That's all I need to know." He doesn't admit what he thinks, though. Which is that the *old* Greg Davis would've thought the rhyming names cute. The *new* Greg Davis, however, is stifling an eye roll.

"We're up." Wes puts his sandwich wrappings in the take-out bag, then shoves his dog's rubber chicken into Greg's hands. "Give a good clucking squeak when I motion you."

Really? This is what Greg's life has come to? Standing in a dog park on his lunch break, squeezing a rubber chicken to squawk and squeak—while watching his Santa Claus father being photographed with a pack of pooches? All while three different women hit on him—on a day he

116

didn't even shave, no less. He gives his whiskered jaw a rub, watching this scene go down as the photographer, camera on tripod, turns to the waiting crowd.

"Ready to cheer on this stately shepherd?" the photographer asks.

Greg looks from him, to Comet—who is sitting at attention beside Santa Claus.

Santa ... aka Pete Davis. Santa who is bent low; his red Santa cap tipped just so; his smiling, white-bearded face near the dog's.

"On three!" the photographer continues, raising his counting fingers to the large, waiting crowd. "One ... two ... *three!*"

"*Woof! Woof!*"

twelve

LINDSEY CAN ALWAYS TELL WHEN it's the dinner hour at the Merry Market. A lull settles in. The Green quiets at this dusky time; lamplight illuminates paned windows in surrounding colonial homes; the number of shoppers dwindles.

Which gives her the perfect excuse to do some of her own shopping.

Yes, she decides later that Tuesday afternoon. It's mid-December already, and time to find a holiday wreath for her tiny house door. So she brings in her old-world Santa from his spot outside her boutique entrance, flips her OPEN sign to CLOSED, bundles up in her coat, hat and mittens, and heads out for a stroll along Main Street. Certainly a nearby garden nursery, or local farm stand, might have fresh balsam wreaths.

Oh, and before locking up her door, there's one more thing to do. It always works when she needs a little direction in her life. Lindsey lifts her snowman snow globe from the shelf and gives it a shake. Sparkling snowflakes twirl like a miniature blizzard blowing beneath the glass.

"*Unsure where to go? Give a little shake ... and your heart will always know,*" she whispers.

And it works. Because after walking only a block along cobblestone sidewalks, Lindsey notices white bulbs strung crisscrossed above the Christmas tree lot at Cooper Hardware. In the evening light, the round bulbs cast a soft glow on rows of fir trees leaning against a long wooden railing. Just beyond, bows of burgundy, and plaid, and gold hang on balsam wreaths lining a multi-level wreath rack.

Hurrying over with her fingers crossed inside her mittens, Lindsey stops at the wreaths decorated with miniature gold balls; or silver jingle bells; or red-berry clusters. But one wreath in particular catches her eye—one with a looped plaid bow and snow-tipped pinecones nestled in its boughs. She lifts the balsam wreath off the rack and tries to picture it on her tiny house door. The bow's long ribbons flutter in a chill breeze as she backs up a step, contemplating the wreath ... *and* backing straight into someone behind her.

"Oh!" she says, spinning around to apologize. "Oh—Dr. *Davis*?" Greg stands there with a trapper hat on his head, his black wool coat hanging open, and—wait, are those whiskers on his face? "I'm so sorry, I didn't see you there!" Lindsey says.

"No, it was my fault," Greg tells her while holding a

tall Christmas tree at arm's length. "I was trying to gauge this for my living room." He looks from Lindsey back to his tree.

"You're getting a tree?"

"Sure am. After long shifts at the hospital, I need to relax and unwind at home." He spins his fresh-cut tree for another scrutiny. "So I like putting out a tree, hanging stockings and garland." He turns to her again. "You know."

"Really?" This is a different side of the gruff, impatient Greg Davis she's come to expect, and one she finds hard to believe. With her free, wreathless hand, Lindsey lifts the brim of her wool beanie and squints closely at him. "*You?* You decorate?"

"I'm a man of many secrets," Greg assures her as he leans his tree back alongside the others against the railing.

"Hey there," another voice calls out. "Lindsey? It's Lindsey, right?"

She and Greg look at the same time to see a man approaching. He wears a gray down jacket, unzipped, over a red flannel shirt and dark jeans. Popcorn spills from a paper cone he's holding. Popcorn which he's diligently munching on.

"Yes …" Lindsey says, stepping closer and slowly smiling. "Wait a minute. I know you from … the post office," she says. "Brian?"

"That's right." He smiles, too, and shakes her mittened hand. "Nice to see you again, Lindsey. Tree shopping today? Maybe for a nice big tree to put all your packages beneath?"

"Oh, those." Lindsey turns to Greg to explain how this kind gentleman held her pile of wrapped packages in the post office, just as they were about to topple from her weighed-down arms. But Greg's moved on to another tree, pulling a balsam fir from the railings. She looks at him a second longer, then turns back to Brian with a shrug. "I'm just buying a wreath today. For my shop door." As she says it, she shivers against another cold gust of wind.

"Popcorn?" Brian asks, holding out the paper cone.

"That's okay." Lindsey shifts her plaid-ribboned wreath to her other hand, and sneaks in another look toward Greg, too.

"It's buttered—and warm," Brian adds. "They have a popcorn machine set up inside the store, in case you want to get out of the cold for a bit."

Lindsey can't miss it, the way this Brian glances over at Greg—as though gauging whether or not he's with her. She actually does the same again, too, tossing Greg another look just as he's finagling a second tree so that he has one in each hand now.

"Well. I won't keep you, Lindsey." Brian gives her a casual wave as he backs up a step or two. "Nice bumping into you again. Maybe I'll see you around."

"You, too. I mean," Lindsey says while also backing up. "I mean, nice seeing you, too!" She gives a mittened wave, then turns to take her wreath to the checkout area set up outside the store. It'll be a relief to get back to her warm house—with no more sideways glances and unexpected bump-ins—and hang her plaid-ribboned wreath on the door.

If she can just get past one particular doctor standing in her direct path. A doctor who has since unsnapped the flaps of his fur-lined trapper hat, and those flaps now hang loose over his ears.

"So." Lindsey stops beside him and considers his two trees. "What kind of tree do you like? Fraser fir?" She reaches out and touches that one, before glancing back at Brian departing. It doesn't escape her that Greg gives a distracted look that way, too.

"Or how about a Scotch pine," Lindsey suggests, "with all those long, gentle needles?"

"Hm?" Greg ponders his two trees and returns the Fraser fir to the rails. "I'm more partial to a balsam. They smell amazing, which is part of the whole Christmas ambiance. You know," he says, dipping his head close to the tree and sniffing the balsam branches, "it makes me feel like I'm out in the woods with all that fresh air, from right inside my condo."

"My tiny house is too small for a tree. It's the one thing I miss most about going tiny. Not having a Christmas tree to decorate. There's room enough for just my Santa and my snowman snow globe."

"Well, that's something, anyway." He sets his balsam tree back with the others, then straightens it when it leans to the side. "I'll still browse, but this one might do the trick. I've got my decorations all waiting."

"You're *trimming* the tree tonight, too?"

He glances at her with a slight nod.

"Aw, you're so lucky." Lindsey hoists her wreath up on her arm. "Well," she says, gazing down the line of trees beneath the strung bulbs crisscrossing the lot, "those are some nice ones, over there," she says, pointing to the right, then turning toward the checkout table. "So … have fun, then!"

"Thanks. You, too," Greg says.

"I will," she calls over her shoulder. "I might even put some ornaments on my … wreath." As she says it, she gives another mittened wave goodbye.

❧

Finally, Greg settles on a six-foot-tall balsam fir. After carrying it to the netting station, Derek Cooper helps him set a blanket across the roof of his Mustang, then strap the tree right on top there.

"Nice car, dude," Derek says. "She's pretty slick."

"Thanks, Coop." Greg knots the rope around the tree, then gives it a yank for good measure. "I'll take you for a cruise in it one of these days."

"And I'm holding you to that," Derek tells him, giving a knock on the roof before waving over the next tree customer's vehicle.

When Greg starts getting inside his Mustang, he notices pine needles and gobs of sticky pine sap all over his black wool coat. "Swell," he mutters while trying to brush off the tiny green needles stuck to the wool fibers.

"Ruined." So he whips off the soiled coat and carefully lays it across the backseat, trying not to get sap on anything inside the car.

As annoyed as he is, all it takes to feel better is turning the key in the ignition and hearing the sound of that engine under the hood. Apparently that V8 purr makes others feel good, too. While coasting through the hardware store's parking lot, a few guys—some alone, some with a girlfriend or wife—give the thumbs-up as his car rumbles past.

Another thing he's noticed the past day or two is the illuminated colonials and Cape Cods on Main Street. Seemingly overnight, Christmas trees now twinkle in living rooms; candles glimmer in paned windows; garland drapes from white picket fences. Yes, Addison is in full holiday mode.

And that Christmas fever is contagious. White cottony faux-snow is tucked into the windows of his favorite coffee shop, Whole Latte Life. In the local toy store's display window, mechanical skaters spin and swoosh on an artificial icy pond surrounded by bottlebrush trees. Fur-caped mannequins stand dressed in long velvet gowns inside the twinkly-light-lined window of Wedding Wishes bridal shop.

Why, if Greg had to say so, Main Street looks straight out of one of Gus' Christmas puzzles—all colorful and sparkling and heartwarming. So when Greg sees the red-and-green Holly Trolley approaching with Gus at the wheel, he can't stop himself from tapping the Mustang's horn in a festive greeting.

The whole scene actually has him whistling a Christmas carol, a familiar *fa-la-la-la-la* filling his car with merriment as he drives by bag-toting shoppers coming out of boutique doors, then turning onto the sidewalk and hurrying along. As he cruises down Main Street toward his condo, though, he notices one woman walking alone. She's huddled into her—wait—her very-familiar-looking shearling-trimmed tan suede coat.

It's Lindsey, and of course she's carrying her newly purchased wreath, too, no doubt on her way back to Vagabond Vintage on the town green.

The sight of her brings Greg's happy whistling to a stop—right when a pang of regret nags at him. Something about Lindsey walking with her wreath strikes Greg as lonely. Her one longing tonight, which she let on to him at Cooper Hardware, was to be able to decorate a tree.

A tree like the one strapped to the top of his Mustang slowly rumbling along Main Street.

A tree he'd planned to decorate *alone*, with Christmas tunes cranking, leftover pizza waiting, heart safe and intact.

But now, this. This sight of Lindsey Haynes stopping his whistled song.

Well now. The old Greg Davis would have pulled right up to the curb beside her in his luxury sedan and invited her to his place. Would have asked her to help decorate his Christmas tree, and maybe have a hot cocoa, too.

Heck, the old Greg Davis would've asked her in the hardware store tree lot, beneath those strung white bulbs, amidst the pine scent of all those fresh-cut evergreens.

But that was the old Greg Davis.

The thing is, the new Greg Davis knows better than to try to plan a fun, romantic evening.

Knows better than to devise a December date. Because that's all he is: a first-date man. All that trying and hoping just leads to the doldrums when the date departs, never to return. That's his thought as his car approaches Lindsey from behind.

But how about this? How about if a night of tree-decorating is completely *unplanned*, and so not a date at all? Now there's a question.

One that has the new Greg Davis pull up alongside Lindsey, stop the car, lean across the front seat and swing open the passenger door—right where she stands on the sidewalk. A gust of icy wind blows inside the warm car. From the driver's seat, Greg bends low and looks out at Lindsey. At her face turned toward him, at her straight blonde bangs hanging from beneath that brimmed wool beanie. At her cheeks flush with the cold. He looks at her for a long, quiet moment.

And then … he does it.

The new Greg Davis simply runs his hand along his whiskered cheek, hitches his head to the empty passenger seat and calls out, "Get in!"

thirteen

STANDING ON THE SIDEWALK, LINDSEY can't quite see inside the black Mustang stopped at the curb. Uncertain, she takes slow steps and squints through the darkness to the car's interior, where a man leans across the front seat and watches her. A man with a whiskered face and wearing a trapper hat with long, floppy earflaps. "*Greg?*" she asks.

"Come on. We'll hang that wreath, then you can help me decorate." He motions her inside the car. "You, well, you should have that Christmas-tree moment." He leans further, looking out from beneath his fur-lined hat. "So get in."

"What about this?" Lindsey holds up her wreath. Its plaid ribbon flutters in that cold wind that won't let up.

"Put it in the backseat, on top of my coat—which is already ruined."

"Oh, no."

Greg nods. "When I carried my tree ... sap, pine

needles, it all made a mess. So come in out of the cold." Again, he motions her into the idling car.

Lindsey takes a step, pauses, then walks quickly to the car, pushes the front seat forward and squeezes behind it to place her wreath on top of Greg's ruined wool coat.

"Okay!" she says with a quick smile when she then settles into the front passenger seat. "Well, thanks. This is a surprise."

"No problem." Greg puts the car in gear and pulls back into traffic.

As they drive down Main Street, Lindsey notices something when they pass several people gathered in a circle while singing and holding sheet music; and when a horse with silver bells on its harness trots by. The rumbling engine of Greg's Mustang actually blocks out all the sounds of Christmas. Inside the insulated car, there are no jingle bells jangling; no carolers' soprano notes soaring high in a melodic *Glo-o-o-o-ria*; no hooves clip-clopping on a holiday horse-and-buggy ride. No Holly Trolley toots.

Inside the car, there is only the rumble of the classic hot rod's engine as Greg downshifts and maneuvers the busy street while heading toward the Merry Market on The Green. Lindsey watches the passing trolley, and singing carolers—hands in muffs, voices open in song— and doesn't hear their sounds.

What's *awkward*, though, is something else. It's the muffled quietness in the car. A quietness more pronounced with each quick glance and small smile between them. Until at last, Greg reaches forward and turns on the car's radio.

"My advice to you this cold night ..." meteorologist Leo Sterling is saying. "Now listen with all your might. Be sure to hold onto your hat. Because the wind will be blowing—this way and that!"

"That jolly weatherman was right," Lindsey says minutes later once they arrive at the Merry Market and stand at her tiny house entrance. She clips a wreath hook over the top of her door, all while the chill wind is swirling leaves and rattling her shop's CLOSED sign.

And getting a coatless Greg to huddle and shiver while standing there holding her large wreath. His flannel shirt alone cannot be keeping him warm, at all.

"You're cold!" Lindsey tells him. "You really can't wear your nice wool coat?"

"No. Believe me, it's wrecked. Those fresh-cut pine trees had lots of oozing sap." He motions to his fur-lined trapper hat then. "But my head's covered, and thirty percent of body heat is lost through the head. So I'm good," he adds while climbing the few stairs to her door and hanging her plaid-ribboned wreath.

"But it's *freezing* out. I must have something that could work for you. Come on inside!" As she says it, she unlocks the door and goes into her tiny house.

When she looks back, Greg's walking past her CLOSED sign, then bends low and almost bumps his head in the doorway. Once inside, he steps around her old-world Santa and stops at her small table, where he sets his trapper hat and drags his hand through his unkempt hair. When he spots her framed corkboard map, he glances at the pushpins pressed along the Eastern Seaboard before turning to her. "Any more pins in your map? Going somewhere new?"

"This time of year, the winter winds steer me south," she explains while considering a rack of clothes. "So after the holidays, I'm heading to a warmer climate, where the roads are clear and it's easier to get around towing my house." She brushes through hangers, sliding sweaters and jackets to the side. "Much as I like a snowy winter night, and curling up inside with that brisk wind blowing, it's tough to maneuver the terrain here in the winter." Another hanger or two later, and she finds it. "Aha!" she says, lifting a jacket off her mini-rack. "It's not wool, and not down-filled ... but with a scarf? It could definitely work," she says, holding up the black leather bomber she picked up at the Christmas trunk sale on the covered bridge. The jacket's leather is aged, and distressed in all the right places.

The funny thing is the way Greg just looks from the jacket, to her, back to the jacket. All without saying a word.

So she takes the jacket off the hanger. "Come on ... Try it on at least!"

Greg walks closer and puts his arms in the sleeves of the jacket she holds. In the tiny house's narrow space, he twists and turns until the jacket's finally on. From behind him, Lindsey hoists it up on his shoulders, then stills. In a moment, she whispers one single word.

"*Perfect.*"

⁓◯

Greg is aware of it all. Of every breath, every fabric rustle, every uttered syllable.

Yes, he hears Lindsey's whisper, and feels the way her hand taps his shoulder after she says, *Perfect*. There's something about being in this space—one that's as cozy as it is confined—that makes every small sound one of magnitude.

"I usually wear wool," he muses while examining the zipper, the front-slash pocket. When he looks up, Lindsey stands there, still in her shearling-trimmed suede coat and brimmed beanie. Her wispy bangs cover her forehead, reaching to her sweet brown eyes.

Oh, no. Back it up. No, no, no. That's noticing *too* many details on this Lindsey Haynes. So the new Greg Davis quickly tugs on a sleeve; twists around to see the jacket's back side. "I never actually had a leather bomber," he says. "But I'll take it."

"You'll need a scarf with it. Because we still have to get to your condo to decorate your tree, and that wind's *really* howling. A scarf will warm you right up." Lindsey heads to a toppling pile of boxes near her clothes rack, pulls out the second box and brushes through several scarves in it.

The thing is? With the whole jacket-swap fiasco, Greg

simply *forgot* about the balsam fir strapped to the roof of his car. So he partially zips his new jacket and waits near the door. In a moment, Lindsey approaches with a burgundy scarf. She loops it around his neck and—surprising him—gently tucks it into the half-zipped jacket, before patting his chest and backing up with a satisfied smile.

Suddenly it's feeling awfully warm in the close quarters of this tiny shop in a tiny house. Colorful fabrics of vintage clothing line the walls; an old Christmas album sits on the record player; swag curtains hang from windows overlooking The Green. Old high-heeled pumps act as bookends to another stack of albums on a shelf above a closet. And that map—with its pushpins—shows all Lindsey's dreamed-of stops. Not to mention her snowman snow globe and old-world Santa adding just the right tiny amount of holiday décor.

Finally, Greg's eyes meet Lindsey's again. Meet her brown eyes, and flushed cheeks.

Well now. The old Greg Davis might have stepped closer, tucked her silky blonde hair behind her ear and leaned in for a little Christmas kiss in this intimate moment.

But instead, the new Greg Davis—standing there in a distressed leather jacket—clears his throat, pulls out his wallet and asks, "What do I owe you for the coat?"

❦

One thing Greg's good for is planning ahead.

Not in the romance department, though. He *used* to do that—scheduling movie nights and lunch dates, buying the right wine, putting his good manners to use—but not anymore. No, all *that* planning has come to a halt this holiday season.

But he *did* haul out his Christmas tree stand earlier. Centered it in front of his two side-by-side paned living room windows. So he and Lindsey get the tree set up in no time.

"This is a nice spot," Lindsey says. "Look, the windows are so big, people will be able to see your tree from the street."

"Those windows are actually replicas of the originals. Twelve-over-twelve panes." Greg switches on a table lamp, which casts a gold hue on the wide-planked hardwood floors. He then brings a string of lights to the tree. "This building was formerly a merchant's grand house, built in 1759. So when it was converted to three condominiums, efforts were made to retain the character. You know … restoring the wood floors, duplicating the millwork. Even historic paint colors were brought in."

"What stories these walls must hold. Very vintage, indeed." Lindsey brushes through a large plastic tote filled with decorations. When she pulls out a tube of gold beads, Greg tells her he doesn't use them.

"They never hang right," he says while tucking the strand of lights into the tree's branches. "And they always look lopsided."

"What?" Lindsey opens the tube and loops the string of gold beads around her arm. "Not if you do it right. There's an *art* to hanging beads," she says while draping them perfectly on the tree, working her way around and around.

Just then, a sudden gust of winter wind rattling the windowpanes has Greg glad to be on *this* side of those windows. As the lights twinkle and Lindsey's gold beads loop, Greg tells her how he imagines colonial life must have been on cold nights like this one.

"Wood-burning fireplaces must've been blazing in candlelit rooms." He glances out to Main Street. "Maybe a horse and buggy clip-clopped past on a dirt road."

And Lindsey, her soft voice chattering, says how glad she is to be having her Christmas-tree moment. "I didn't think I'd actually have one this year. It's my first Christmas in a tiny house, so I was really missing this, well, this *tradition*," she says while lifting an ornament out of the tote.

As she does, another gust of wind rattles the window and gets the lights flickering, too. *On, off.* On a little longer, then? Darkness.

"Oh, no!" Lindsey cries.

"It's all right," Greg says in the shadows. He glances out the window to see that the entire street has gone black. "Don't move, I'll get a light."

He steps out from behind the balsam fir and feels his way to the kitchen. The thing is—and doesn't he know it—the old Greg Davis would've grabbed matches and lit

134

several candles, setting them down here on an end table, and there on the mantel. The flickering candlelight would make for a very romantic opportunity with the power out on this cold night.

But, nope. Greg's sticking to his guns and employing all his resolve to protect his heart.

The new Greg Davis instead gets a flashlight from the pantry closet, then shines the beam on an upholstered chair for Lindsey. Once she sits, he turns his flashlight onto the tote and lifts out a box of woodland ornaments, which he sets on the sofa. Finally, he puts the flashlight on an end table and points the beam toward the partially decorated tree.

"This work okay?" he asks Lindsey in near darkness.

"It'll do," she admits with a glance toward the rattling window. "I guess Leo Sterling was right. What a windy night!"

When she stands to continue decorating, as quickly as the lights went out, they flicker and flash on once again. This time, they hold steady.

"Hooray," Lindsey says, taking in the room bathed in golden lamplight. And it's as if she's seeing it now for the first time. She wanders over to look at an old snowy painting of a babbling brook; drags a fingertip across his small cherry desk tucked into an alcove; turns on a floor lamp beside the sofa; admires a large piece of tatted lace that's framed behind glass; crosses the threadbare Oriental rug on her way back to the tree.

Funny, but it feels as if Greg's seeing Lindsey for the

first time, too. She wears a navy cable-knit sweater over pale gray skinny jeans. Her silver stud earrings shimmer; her smile comes easy while tree decorating. Really, no one prettier has ever stood in his living room before.

"Well," Greg says while snapping off the flashlight, and while thinking ... *Enough of that*. "Before the power goes out again with all this wind, I'd better find us something to eat."

"Do you need any help?"

"No, I'm good," he calls over his shoulder, right before opening the refrigerator to see what's to be had. Of course, the old Greg Davis would put out cheese and crackers, not to mention a bottle of wine.

But that was the old Greg Davis, the one who wore a long black wool coat and drove a luxury sedan.

The new Greg Davis—the one who wears a leather bomber now and drives a '68 Mustang—pulls out a platter of leftover pizza slices from Luigi's and heats them in the microwave. Grabbing a couple of paper plates and a bag of chips, he puts it all unceremoniously on the coffee table in the living room. This new Greg Davis doesn't even pour the potato chips into a bowl to set a halfway-decent atmosphere. No, he just rips open the bag.

"Dig in," he says when he returns from the kitchen— not with two crystal goblets and a bottle of fine wine, but instead with red plastic cups and a jug of soda.

This casual vibe—with the tree somewhat decorated, and their coats tossed over a chair back, and yesterday's mail shoved aside on the coffee table—it's all, well, it's *easy*. This way, no effort ... no letdown. So when Lindsey slips off her ankle boots and settles on a cushion on the floor beside the coffee table, Greg sits on the edge of the couch. From there, he shoves up his shirtsleeves and pours the soda. The surprising thing is—paper plates and plastic cups and all—he doesn't really mind it.

And with the way Lindsey lifts the biggest, gooiest slice of pizza, apparently neither does she.

Later, Greg reaches for the box of woodland animal ornaments beside him on the couch. "My father whittled most of these," he says while setting a squirrel and a raccoon on the coffee table. Diligent knife strokes depict the animals' fur patterns, the turn of their ears, the curve of their paws. "These are the only ornaments I put on my tree."

"No shiny bells and sparkling glass balls?"

Greg shakes his head and sets down a pair of wooden deer, along with a carved pine tree. "Just these."

Lindsey lifts one of the deer—a pretty doe covered with silver glitter meant to look like icy snow.

"Did you know that snow won't melt on a deer's back?" Greg asks.

"It doesn't?"

"No. Their fur has such insulating qualities, no heat gets through it to melt the snow."

"Well, I'll be," Lindsey says, setting aside the doe and lifting a carved chipmunk. "Now these are charming! Would your father happen to be Pete ... of Near and Deer fame?"

"That's the one."

"Small world. Well—small town! I met him at the Merry Market the other day. Stopped at his booth and placed an order for two deer, for my parents." She runs her hand along the whittled chipmunk's grooves and notches. "So did your father teach you to whittle, too?"

Greg sets down a larger buck with sweeping antlers. "He tried. But my brother, Wes, is the whittler. I don't like to handle knives like that and risk injuring my hands. You know, with doing surgery and all."

"Totally get it," Lindsey says as she stands. "I cannot *wait* to hang these." She scoops up some carved birds, a bear, rabbits and the deer, then squints at the tree.

"Wait." Greg takes a quick bite of another slice of pizza, then walks to a tabletop lamp. "I'll turn off these lights," he says around the food, "so that just the tree lights shine. It's easier to decorate that way, seeing the animals lit up on the tree as you hang them."

Lindsey lifts a white wooden rabbit with tall, straight ears and loops it onto a middle branch. "I think so, too," she says while stepping back and considering the birch bunny.

Slowly, then, the animals get hung: a striped chipmunk here, a masked raccoon there. Greg, finger to chin, steps aside on the navy-and-burgundy Oriental rug and looks for an empty spot on the tree. Meanwhile, with a whittled squirrel in hand, Lindsey backs around the tree as Greg lifts a deer and goes to the other side. He presses down branches, moves some twinkling lights. Those lights cast a soft glow on the living room; on the gold walls and wide white crown molding; on the Tiffany lamp atop a mahogany pedestal table.

They both concentrate on finding just the right spot to hang their whittled animals. Holding one up high, trying one tucked low, all while backing slowly around the tree … it happens again.

Yes, another collision ensues. Another accidental, unintentional run-in, its impact as surprising as all the others—starting with a tiny house hitting Greg's car, to their elbow-bumping at Gus' dinner, to their colliding while Christmas-tree-and-wreath shopping. Each and every time, the physical contact resulted in a jolted withdrawal.

This time, they back right into each other on the window side of the big balsam fir.

But *this* time, they don't pull away. Instead, they stop, turn and look at each other.

In the dim twinkling light, Lindsey whispers, "*Greg.*"

Greg, holding his whittled deer, steps closer and whispers, "*Lindsey.*" He reaches a hand to touch her soft, blonde hair. At the very same time, she stretches up on tiptoe to lean in close. And it's all perfect, Greg convinces himself, because none of this was planned. It just is … happening.

And now, a kiss is about to.

About to, until … *Beep! Beep! Beep!*

In a flash, they both jump back, startled by that sharp, intrusive noise. Lindsey drops her squirrel ornament, and when she bends to pick it up, bumps right into the tree.

"Oh," Greg says while unclipping a small pager from his belt. "It's the hospital calling me. One of my patients had an emergency." In the tree's glow, he squints to read a line of text on the pager's screen.

When he glances over at Lindsey, she's hung the squirrel on the tree and is pressing down a mussed piece of her hair, all while stealing a glance at Greg.

He gives himself one moment—just one—to watch her beside the twinkling tree. She stands there stocking-footed in her jeans and sweater. A simple pearl pendant hangs from her neck.

Then he gives another look at the pager before clipping it back on his belt. Shaking his head regretfully, he tells Lindsey, "I've got to go. I'm sorry. Can I drop you off at your house on the way?"

"Oh, no. That's okay." As she says it, Lindsey is suddenly crossing the living room. "Your patient needs you, you're busy." All the while, she's pulling on her black ankle boots, pushing her arms into her suede coat's sleeves, and tugging on her brimmed beanie. Tugging it low, it seems, to conceal the disappointment in her eyes, maybe? Or the pink flush of her cheeks? She gives a quick smile and wave before rushing toward the back door off the kitchen. "I'm parked just across the street on The Green anyway. And thanks," she calls. "It's been fun!"

Greg looks from his pager again to Lindsey flying in a blur out the door. He follows behind her and watches as she runs across the back porch and hurries down a flight of wooden stairs, her boots clumping on each step.

"Lindsey!" he yells.

But in the brisk, blowing wind, she's out of earshot, and when she rounds the corner, he loses sight of her. But he imagines she's on The Green in only moments, zigging and zagging between the other vendors and evening shoppers. She'd be headed to her tiny house, of course. Her beloved shop-on-wheels where just hours ago, they'd hung her plaid-ribboned wreath.

Still looking toward The Green, Greg figures that right about now, the wreathed door on her little shingled house is sweeping open. Lindsey might be rushing inside and switching on a light, maybe nearly tripping over her old-world Santa—before finally closing up shop and returning to Snowflake Lake in the cold night.

Standing there with his hands on the porch railing, he looks out toward the distant Merry Market. It's so obvious: Lindsey was as caught off guard by their unintentional tree-decorating collision as he was.

But you see? One near-romantic moment by a twinkling Christmas tree, and *already* his heart is getting ideas of its own.

And it's just not worth it. In mere weeks, footloose-and-pretty Lindsey Haynes and her tiny house will be toodling down the highway, straight out of Addison and straight out of his life, too.

fourteen

A FEW HOURS LATER, GREG takes off his surgical gloves, gown and mask outside the operating room. The surgery went well, and for that he's thankful. But now that it's behind him, he realizes the surgery served another purpose: It kept thoughts of Lindsey at bay.

Now? Those thoughts are back. He walks over to the large sink. "Seriously? 'Tis the season to be jolly?" he quietly asks himself as water runs from the faucet. "More like 'tis the season to be sorry," he adds while pressing the soap dispenser and scrubbing his hands and arms over the sink. No matter that he just came out of a successful surgery; no matter that the hospital is busy this late at night; no matter that he's hungry and ready to go find something to eat.

None of that matters.

The only thing on his mind now is the vision of how *close* he came to kissing Lindsey Haynes. Free-spirited, footloose Lindsey. How very close he came to touching her hair, leaning in and pressing his lips to hers beside a twinkling Christmas tree.

Which would lead to only one thing, just like it did the past three years with Vera first, then Jane, followed by Penny. Holiday heartbreak. He'd had a dance with one, lunch with the other, an *almost* movie night with the third. Until someone *else* swooped in and swept each of those lovely ladies right off their feet.

Heaven knows he can't change the past; he can only protect himself from that dreaded seasonal sadness by staying single. Love has never been in the Christmas cards for him. It won't be this year, either, as Lindsey will be picking up the highway out of Addison in just weeks. So it's important he stick to his resolve to remain single and pain free.

"Stupid, stupid, stupid," Greg says with each soapy scrub.

If anything might make him feel better, it's a hot meal. Somehow the couple of leftover pizza slices he ate earlier were merely a snack. So in the hospital cafeteria, he grabs a Salisbury steak with mashed potatoes and gravy—green beans on the side—and carries his tray to a seat. A few coworkers linger with coffee or a sandwich at random tables. Greg nods at the familiar faces, but opts for an empty table where a day-old newspaper is strewn about. Maybe yesterday's headlines will distract him from his Lindsey thoughts.

First he digs into his gravy-and-mushroom steak, though, dragging a hunk of it through his mashed potatoes before lifting it all to his mouth. Still, something's nagging at him as he reaches for the front page. One bothersome thought nips at him like a pesky dog.

And it's this: That near-kiss should *never* have happened.

Because the *new* Greg Davis rewrote the rules of romance. Rules he abided by tonight when he was *sure* to give *no* attention to detail. There was no wine, no cheese. And *no* candles setting a romantic mood, that's for darn sure. Nope, he was keeping romance out of the picture and was all flashlights and paper plates instead.

And Lindsey was *into* that?

"Hey, Doc Davis," another surgeon says while walking past. "Season's greetings."

Greg simply gives a head nod, thinking to himself that it's been one long night, from start—at the Christmas tree lot—to finish.

A nurse approaches, but hurries right by, squeezing between two round tables beside him. "Get some shut-eye for Friday, Dr. Davis! You're looking a little fatigued."

Friday—don't remind him. It's the day of his upcoming auction. Beneath the harsh cafeteria lighting, he ignores the nurse's remark and lifts a forkful of green beans, then straightens a section of newspaper in front of him.

Not that he's reading it.

How can he? Instead he's thinking that out of the goodness of his heart, he did something special: He created one Christmas-tree moment for Lindsey. And what did it do? It led straight to that near-kiss. A near-kiss beside a decorated tree in a dark living room all primed for a romantic interlude with its shadows and dimly glowing lights. With its cold wind rapping at the windowpanes.

Yes, one hour of tree-decorating got him right back into the snare of a merry mess ... with a footloose daydreamer. A daydreamer whose home is on *wheels*, for crying out loud.

After he swore off any female entanglements this holiday season, how can this be happening?

"It's not," he mutters while slicing his fork through a hunk of Salisbury steak.

"What?" another passing doctor asks. He wears a white lab coat with enough wrinkles in it to indicate the inordinate length of the poor man's day. "You say something?" he asks Greg as he slows, hot coffee in hand, and pushes a rogue cafeteria chair closer to a table.

Greg waves him off and instead digs into that gravy-laden steak again.

One holiday-decorating hour led to a near-*miss* kiss. *Miss* being the operative word.

Dragging a forkful of green beans through the meat-and-potato jumble on his plate, now more than ever, Greg's thankful for his pager. Ultimately, with a few loud chirps, its shrill beeping saved the season. That precious pager prevented a clandestine Christmas calamity, leaving his heart intact.

Okay, so it's time to get a grip, take a breath and

reassert. He pushes his tray of dishes back and inhales deeply. No more Lindsey, no more holiday moments. To sidestep any seasonal sadness, he only needs to get through the next few weeks—that's all—single and solo.

Because if there's one thing orthopedic surgeon Greg Davis knows, it's this: Bones will mend, fractures heal. But you can never put a cast around a broken heart.

⌒∿○

Lindsey thought it would never happen, but it has.

After driving her tiny house back to its spot between two pine trees at Snowflake Lake, comfort returns. It took a while, though. It took feeling shaken up inside first, and actually trembling when she rushed away from Greg's condominium. But that all subsides as she settles into her cozy tiny home, puts on a flannel sleepshirt over thermal leggings, has a cup of hot tea while her heartbeat slows, then climbs the ladder to her loft.

And lies there in her bed.

Lies there with visions of Greg Davis dancing in her head. Visions of his scruffy, unshaven face; his leather bomber seeming custom-made for his strong shoulders; his Mustang Fastback—so *very* vagabond. His nonchalance.

Her eyes open with the thought of their near-miss kiss as they hung whittled ornaments of rabbits and carved deer on his Christmas tree.

Right. Then she *bolted* like a deer into the thicket, is what she did.

Unable to sleep, she gingerly steps down the loft ladder—then proceeds to stub her toe while moving around a pile of vintage clothing waiting to be inventoried in her shop.

"Ooh, ooh, ooh," she exclaims, limping to her kitchenette and pouring herself a glass of water. Her framed map hangs over the table, and while hobbling on one foot, Lindsey notices something a bit alarming. In fact, she has to stop and study that corkboard map to be sure.

Okay, so it's true. She hasn't pressed in *any* new pushpins since arriving in Addison. Not one. This is so unlike her, as she's *always* plotting new destinations. New places, new adventures!

So she picks up a green pin—green signifying where she'd *like* to go—and looks at the map.

"Hmm. I'm not sure," she says while dropping the pin into her pin mug. "I need a walk to clear my thoughts." She nods to herself. "Yes, then I'll know."

Sliding a box of 1950s gloves and hats to beneath her table, she makes room to dress warmly: après ski boots over her thermal leggings; parka, with fur-trimmed hood pulled up tight around her head. Thankfully, Gus' lantern is still here, too. She'll take it outside with her for a moonlit walk to the lakeside bench—the one where her uncle always leaves a thick, fluffy blanket.

One thing living on the road has taught Lindsey? Her best thinking happens by water—be it the sea, a lake or cove. Doesn't matter. As long as there are little waves rippling and lapping, that soothing sound brings a clarity to her worries.

She walks beneath the moonlight, which shines on a lacy fringe of ice around the lake. Off to the side, curling woodsmoke rises from the chimneys of Wren Den, Mockingbird Manor and Hawk Hut. And the towering lakeside Christmas tree is fully illuminated with twinkling lights that also cast a glow on the surrounding scenery.

Once on the bench, Lindsey tugs that thick blanket over her lap. The blanket's warmth calms her thoughts.

For a moment, anyway.

Until she sighs when, in this hushed spot, she thinks only of one particular pager loudly beeping.

"It was probably all for the best," she whispers. Across the lake, a deer stands near a tall maple tree, its branches stark against the moonlit sky. There's still a little snow on the ground, but the wind has finally died down. It's very peaceful here, unlike the last, sudden chaos-filled minutes in Greg's living room.

Yes, Lindsey decides while thinking of her hurried exodus from Greg's home; while remembering her breathless rushing across The Green to her tiny house. They can simply wash their hands of each other and go their separate ways. No kiss ... no entanglements. Because, well, this is Greg's home. From her lakeside bench, she throws a glance back at her tiny house between two tall pines.

"And I'm still free to roam," she quietly reminds herself, sitting alone in the night's long shadows.

fifteen

BY FRIDAY, ALL THOUGHTS OF Greg Davis are out of Lindsey's mind. Because between being busier than she's ever been in her tiny boutique set up at the Merry Market, and with plans to bid on that must-have 1960s wedding gown at the historical society, there's no room left for *any* other thoughts.

There's no room left in her tiny house, either, when a customer opens the shop door and bumps it into a rack of handbags. Lindsey can barely contain her one-of-a-kind inventory—and her eager shoppers crowding in, too! With the calendar days ticking closer and closer to Christmas, customers keep surging into Vagabond Vintage. It's so busy, she moves her snowman snow globe to a higher shelf just for safekeeping.

Meanwhile, items are selling like, well … like hot cocoa on a snowy day. She can't keep her vintage clothing on the racks. People stream in and warm up with a quick "*Brrr!*" After rubbing their cold hands together, they turn those hands on a scalloped-hem poncho; brown herringbone bell-bottoms; a tooled-leather purse; a khaki pearl-snap shirt; suede cowboy boots; a macramé plant hanger; framed pressed flowers. And gloves—leather, buttoned and cuffed. Hats, too—knitted, pom-pommed and stocking style.

Each and every guy and gal also admires Lindsey's tiny house. The questions keep coming as the customers browse and shop.

I've never been in a tiny house. Do you live here, too?
Is there a dressing room where I can try this on?
This is your real house? So cool!
Do you offer giftwrapping?
You actually drive this tiny house around?

With each answer—each nod assuring that yes, this is her home; and each point directing to the cramped dressing room behind the curtain—Lindsey steals a glance outside to the big, ticking town square clock. Garland wraps up its tall post, right to the gold Roman numerals on the clock's ornate face. The last thing she wants to do is miss out on bidding for that vintage wedding gown at the historical society auction. Because that gown would be absolutely ideal for her shop.

Another glance.

And it's getting late! The auction starts at seven o'clock, and bloomin' heck … it's seven now!

Left with no choice, Lindsey nudges out her last

customer, one who reaches for a neatly folded pile of retro blue jeans. "Oh!" the woman exclaims. "But … but …"

"Merry Market is offering a free giftwrap table *tomorrow*," Lindsey tries to persuade the persistent customer. "Please come back then," Lindsey says, tugging on the woman's arm and pointing her to the door. "When I'll have *new* treasures."

At last, quiet. An empty shop. Lindsey brings in her old-world Santa, grabs her coat and hat, flips over her CLOSED sign and rushes straight down Main Street's cobblestone sidewalk. Pulling on her slouchy beanie as she goes, she scoots around shoppers this way, brushes past carolers that way. If only she can get to the auction in time! That lacy wedding gown would look stunning hanging on her black dress form. Why, she even has a faux-fur stole to drape over it.

Spotting the historical society building only blocks away now, she gives another glance to her wristwatch. The minutes are ticking! Ahead, mobs of people are milling about. Cars overflow from the parking lot. By the time Lindsey gets to the entrance, flies up the stairs and pushes through the wreathed double doors, it's seven thirty. She's missed the first half hour.

In a blur, she breezes to the reception desk, grabs auction paddle number seventy-five and hurries off.

Only to do an about-face a moment later, even as she's hearing the auctioneer chant in the bidding room.

"Oh, miss," the receptionist calls to her. "You have to *register* your paddle."

151

"What?" Lindsey asks while spinning around.

The receptionist nods and pushes a registration card across the countertop. "You can't bid without us having your name and particulars." She sets a pen on top of the card.

So Lindsey does it. The problem is, while bent over and filling out the paddle-card with her name and contact information, the auctioneer's chant continues.

Eighty dollars. Now one hundred. One hundred. One hundred. One twenty now. One twenty. Do I hear one thirty? Going, going … gone! Sold for one hundred thirty dollars to paddle number forty-two.

Though discouraged, Lindsey does whatever she can—crossing her fingers and knocking on wood—to will that the wedding gown *not* be the item that just sold.

With the paperwork complete, she finally picks up her paddle number seventy-five again, breathlessly turns and runs down the hallway to the auction room. The whole way, a new rapid-fire bidding chant grows louder with each step.

"*Wait!*" she calls out. Her brimmed beanie sits lopsided on her head, her shearling-lined coat is open and flapping behind her. Golly gumdrops, if she doesn't act fast, she's going to miss out on that vintage wedding gown!

Turning into the mobbed auction room, she sees wall-to-wall folding chairs. Each and every seat is filled. Pushing her way through the crowd, Lindsey leans to the side for a glimpse of the proceedings. On stage, the first thing that catches her eye is over on the left. It's an antique tambour mantel clock with a *Sold!* ticket already on it. Next in the lineup is a boxed set of classic Christmas

152

ornaments from Snowflakes and Coffee Cakes.

"Oh, shoot!" Lindsey exclaims under her breath. That *also* has a *Sold!* ticket on it.

Quickly, quickly, her eyes continue scanning the items. Next is a local author's collection of signed novels ... Also already sold.

Almost without hope, suddenly Lindsey thinks that if it were possible, this is the moment she might hear a heavenly choir sing.

Because there—center stage—is her small miracle.

The item she's been waiting for is nicely illuminated by a spotlight above so that it actually *looks* angelic: The ivory satin-and-lace 1960s wedding gown drapes from a mannequin. A mannequin also wearing the accompanying pillbox hat with netting.

Even better? There is not a *Sold!* sticker to be seen anywhere on the gown.

Which sets off a new panic. Because all around her, paddles are rising, then falling. Rising, falling. Then again. Rising in persistent and constant bids. Not only that, but in some sort of auction frenzy, the auctioneer is also chanting a mile a minute.

One hundred. One fifteen. Now one twenty. Do I hear one twenty-five?

A woman in a buffalo-plaid sheath stands and thrusts up her paddle. "One *forty*," she yells, clearly *and* firmly. Okay, it's obvious that this bidder won't stand for losing out on the item. Her tone dares *anyone* to outbid her, and if they do, well might she just paddle *them*, instead.

"One hundred … *fifty!*" Lindsey finds herself yelling while waving her paddle. "Yes, one fifty!"

The auctioneer looks to her standing in the aisle. "*Sold,*" he declares with a bang of his gavel, "to paddle number seventy-five!"

"Woo-hoo! I got it." Lindsey gives her paddle a celebratory twirl.

"Please, young lady," the auctioneer continues. "Step right up to claim your prize: dinner and a carriage ride on a romantic date with Addison's *most* eligible bachelor … Dr. Gregory Davis!"

A ton of bricks might as well have swung right at her. Because those particular words are all it takes to stop Lindsey in her tracks as she lowers her paddle. Still not getting the full view of the stage from the crowded aisle, she calls out, "*What?*"

"Your dinner has been donated by Cedar Ridge Tavern, and carriage ride is courtesy of Cooper Hardware," the auctioneer concludes while waving Lindsey toward the stage.

But still, her feet won't move. Standing there frozen, instead something else happens.

Whispers. Whispers rise from all around her, getting her to turn this way, first, then that way.

You go, girl, and *Shucks, this auction's rigged*, and *Lucky you, hon!*

Then another voice, this one the auctioneer's again. "Step right up to claim your prize," he announces while holding up a *Sold!* sticker.

Someone finally gives Lindsey a nudge, so she stumbles a few steps forward and looks to the right side of the stage where a man stands. A man wearing an *awfully* familiar leather bomber.

A man with a shadow of whiskers on his face; with light brown hair reaching to his collar. He's got on black jeans, too. Yes … standing there with his arms crossed over his chest is Greg Davis.

Greg Davis, standing beside a blank cardboard cutout of a simple female shape.

❧

It's warm beneath the stage lights. That bright heat gets Greg to shift his staid stance as he looks out into the sea of bidding faces. The room buzzes with tense energy as all heads turn to see precisely *who* holds the winning paddle. Everyone's looking toward the back of the room as the winner slowly makes her way down the center aisle. Murmurs rise in the now-quieting space. People move aside to leave a clear path, almost like a runway, for the winning bidder.

Greg wonders if the bid came from someone he knows.

Or maybe this year, it'll be a perfect stranger—just bidding for charity's sake.

Finally, the winner comes into view. There's her booted leg, her tan coat. From the stage, he leans forward and squints. Her slouchy, brimmed beanie on top of her long, blonde hair.

"Wait a minute." Greg shakes his head, looks away, then back again. "Oh, *no*."

❧

Lindsey continues walking down the aisle. Her shearling-lined coat hangs limp now. In her hand, slack by her side, is her winning paddle.

The room quiets.

When Lindsey clearly spots Greg, she actually blushes. A red heat moves up to her flushed cheeks as the auctioneer encourages her. He motions her closer while holding out that *Sold!* sticker.

"But. But … the gown," Lindsey stammers while climbing the few steps to the stage and pointing to the gorgeous lace wedding gown. "I thought …"

"No," the auctioneer informs her. "The gown sold just before your date with the good doctor."

"But there's no sold ticket on it?"

"The gown is antique, and the fabric is much too delicate," the auctioneer kindly explains.

Then? Well, then he takes her arm and leads her to Greg—all while Lindsey turns her head to watch that coveted vintage gown diminish with each reluctant step she takes away from it.

❧

With his leather-jacket-clad arms still crossed, Greg glares at Lindsey. The moment is even more humiliating than he'd expected. Especially when the auctioneer approaches and moves aside the full-sized cardboard female cutout, then motions for Lindsey to stand in its place beside Greg.

Next comes the ultimate insult: The auctioneer gives Lindsey a *Sold!* sticker.

"Tell me you didn't do this," Greg manages to say through the side of his mouth.

"I didn't." Lindsey turns to him with her sticker, her eyes searching for a spot to place it. "It's not what you're thinking," she says while pressing it to his shoulder. "I *thought* I was bidding on the gown. You know … for my shop."

"Didn't you *see* me?"

"No! I was late. And there were *hordes* of women— sitting, jumping up with paddles, blocking the way. I'm only five feet tall and couldn't see."

With his knuckles to his jaw, Greg leans closer to Lindsey and talks through clenched teeth. "I can't believe you actually bid on me. You *knew* how much I was dreading this night. Are you rubbing it in or something?"

"Honestly," Lindsey whispers back. "It's all an … an *accident*."

"Please. *Another* one?" Greg glances across the stage. "Can't talk now. The photographer is taking pictures, so … smile. We'll talk more on our *arranged* date."

"When? It's not tomorrow, is it? There are so many Merry Market festivities planned."

"Tuesday. This Tuesday. Which gives the media enough time to get pictures and an article in the following week's *Addison Weekly*."

Lindsey steps closer beside him, stretches up and whispers in his ear. "We don't have to *go* on the date. It's okay," she says, looking directly at him. "It's all a misunderstanding. So I'll just pay for my bid and everyone goes off happy. No need for further dealings, and we say goodbye."

Greg gives a light laugh. It's laced with regret, and maybe a little hopelessness. "Oh, no. No, no, no. You don't get it, Miss Haynes. This annual date is an all-out media blitz. So steel yourself."

The photographer stops in front of the winner of the signed-novel collection and tells the woman, "Smile!"

Greg watches, thinking that this year? This year he didn't want a holiday romance. No matter what, he'd vowed to stay romance-free and keep his heart intact. Yet the more he resisted romance, the more it's been snowballing ... growing with this bid date tonight into a Christmas avalanche of agita.

Now the photographer moves in front of Greg and Lindsey. He lifts his camera and takes aim.

Oh, doesn't Greg know the routine. Lean just right, smile just so. Give them what they want. And the old Greg Davis, the one who'd have been standing there in his sweater vest and chinos, well, he'd have given a megawatt smile and put his arm around Lindsey's petite shoulders.

But this is the new Greg Davis. The one who will never do a fund-raising auction again.

The one who, in his black leather bomber and jeans, hooks his finger in a belt loop and barely gives a *half* smile. As he glances down at Lindsey wrapping her hand around his leather-clad arm, she leans into him and manages what he can't—a wide smile for the camera.

sixteen

Two WHITE, SLATTED-WOOD ROCKERS SIT on Cardinal Cabin's front porch. Red-and-blue tartan throws are draped over each chair, making them the perfect lakeside spot for girl talk. You can see the serene lake and surrounding woods, cup a mug of hot cocoa close and … spill the beans.

Saturday morning, that's the first thing Lindsey does. She bundles up in her slouchy beanie and suede coat, treks to her new friend's cabin and *rat-a-tat-tats* the woodpecker doorknocker on the wood-planked door. In true girlfriend style, Penny sees her distress and brings out two hot cocoas doused with marshmallows.

"Oh, Penny," Lindsey begins while clasping the warm mug with her mittened hands. "You'll never believe what I did. I could barely sleep last night, it's that awful."

"Come on." Penny, in a navy parka, reaches over and pats her arm. "It can't be that bad."

"It is. It's so bad, I can't even show myself around

town. Seriously, it'll be hard to face my customers at the Merry Market later today. So many of them probably saw what I did last night."

"What *happened*? Just tell me."

The last thing Lindsey needs is for anyone else to hear her story. So she looks around and sees Penny's guy, Frank, who's busy at his chopping block splitting wood for the cabins' fireplaces. *Whack! Thunk!* comes the sound of his axe.

In the other direction, Lindsey spots her uncle Gus. Problem is, Gus is a *little* too close as he supposedly fills a nearby bird feeder hanging from a maple tree branch. With the way he's positioned himself in his wool jacket and newsboy cap, it could look like he's got an ear turned to them, doing a little eavesdropping, maybe?

So Lindsey leans to Penny on the rocker beside her and cups Penny's ear. "I gave the highest bid …"

"You *didn't*," Penny says a minute later.

Lindsey only nods.

"Now that's one way to get a guy's attention!" Penny exclaims.

Lindsey presses a finger to her pursed lips. "Shh." She glances at Gus again. Beyond him, sunlight sparkles on the gentle ripples of Snowflake Lake. "But I'm telling you that I didn't *intend* to bid on Greg. I thought … oh, I'm so embarrassed. I *thought* I was bidding on a vintage wedding gown from Wedding Wishes. You know, because lots of my customers might get a Christmas proposal, then come to me for a dress."

"Sure, Linz," Penny says with a twinkle in her eye as

she sips her cocoa. "*Sure*. But I still think it's kind of sweet. And I'll bet Greg's actually glad! He gets a date with someone he already knows."

"You don't understand." Again Lindsey throws another quick glance Gus' way, noticing he's moved to *this* side of Penny's cardinal bird feeder as he lifts a scoop of black-oil sunflower seeds. "Greg and I keep *ridiculously* bumping into each other, again and again," Lindsey says in a low voice. "First the car accident. Then, well … we really just keep finding ways to annoy each other."

Penny tucks her copper-colored hair behind an ear and looks closely at Lindsey. "Is it annoyance?" she asks. "Or … a spark?"

"What?"

"Yup. A spark, which turns into a fire of passion you can't deny!"

"Penny *Hart*!"

"No, listen." Penny sips her cocoa. Then she sets the cup down beside a gray milk can filled with green pine boughs on a table beside her. "I have experience with this," she explains, pointing to Frank at the tree-stump chopping block. "Last year, Frank and I kept crossing paths, too. I couldn't sleep—just like you—wondering about Frank and our relationship. Until ol' softie," she whispers now, "*Gus*, planted us beneath the mistletoe, where Frank and I kissed. I mean, we … *kissed*," she says with a smile, then digs her cell phone from her parka pocket, pulls off her mittens and scrolls through her photos. "Look," she says showing a photograph of her

162

and Frank in a swoon-worthy embrace. "Long story, but that picture ended up being featured in my holiday promo at work last winter. And more importantly, Linz? After that kiss, Frank and I just *knew* we were destined to be together."

"Really?"

Penny nods with an unmistakable twinkle in her eye. "It was all in the kiss."

"What are you saying?"

"You need a kiss from Dr. Davis. One kiss that'll give you an answer. And then, you'll know."

"Know what?"

"If it's annoyance between you two." Penny hesitates, her pause giving just the right dramatic effect. "Or … if it's love."

Not expecting those words, Lindsey practically chokes on her hot cocoa. "I only met him two *weeks* ago!" she sputters.

To which Penny sits back in her white rocker and shrugs. Beyond, a cardinal flitters onto a low pine branch and hops closer, as though it's listening in. "One little kiss is all it takes," Penny continues in a flirty tone. "Then there'll be no more sleepless nights because … you'll *know.*"

"It's the busiest day here yet," Pete says. He's standing in his Near and Deer booth, arranging whittled and glittered deer on tufts of faux cottony snow. Behind him, a wall shelf is lined with other carved woodland animals: foxes, squirrels, beavers. "This Merry Market was a great idea for the town."

After ringing out another customer—this one buying a matched doe-and-buck set—Greg glances out at The Green. People walk about in parkas and jackets; in earmuffs and pom-pommed beanies; holding shopping bags and cups of hot cocoa. "Sheesh, Dad. Look at the crowds."

"Well sure, son. Saturdays are mobbed. Folks come for the free candy canes from elves and costumed reindeer, and for the wandering carolers singing jolly jingles. Plus don't forget the complimentary giftwrap station," Pete says while pointing to a long table covered with boxes of bows and rolls of wrapping paper. Several teens in elf costumes sit on one side, scissors and tape in hand as they cut and unroll and fold paper corners over gift boxes. A large sign beside the table reads: *Save Time For Yourself! Free Giftwrap From an Elf!*

Candy? Wrapped presents? Carolers holding sheet music in their hands?

Greg sees none of it. No, all he's seen since he got here midafternoon is one distinct, shingled tiny house parked at the far side of The Green. It's as though he's got some sort of festive-fixation on it. Apparently he's not the only one, either, from the looks of the milling crowd. Lindsey must've won over all the hearts of Addison because everyone on The Green seems to be wearing something vintage—stocking hats, fur-trimmed capes, fringed scarves, embroidered leather gloves.

"But mostly," Pete continues, "I think it's a visit from Santa Claus that brings the crowds."

"Well, I cleared my schedule," Greg says, "and am ready to cover your booth for your Santa shift."

Pete picks up a handful of papers from beneath the cashbox. "Oh, shoot. I still have a ton of orders for notched pine trees. Got to get these done, first."

"No, you can't." Greg looks over to the North Pole Station ... and at the line of people leading up to it. Children hold the hands of parents who are searching side to side for Santa. Those eager parents are checking their watches, and bending to assure their anxious tots. "Old man Cooper clocked out from his Santa duty already, Dad. The Santa chair is empty." Greg points to the large green velvet chair that is glaringly vacant. "Looks bad. You're up next to sit in that chair and play Old Saint Nick—and you're not even dressed!" he says, giving a once-over to Pete's fleece-lined green jacket, fingerless gloves and dark wool cap. "You better get in costume, pronto."

Pete steps out of the booth, cranes his neck past the crowd and shakes his head. "Shoot," he whispers when he looks back at Greg. "Can't *you* whittle my little trees? It's easy, son." As he says it, a young couple stops and browses the carved deer sprinkled with snow-like silver glitter. So Pete rushes back in the booth and yanks Greg close. "The orders don't stop today! I need help, because they all want the little trees on their mantels *with* the deer."

"You know I can't whittle and risk injuring my hands," Greg manages while counting out change.

Pete squints long at Greg, who begins wrapping up the glittered deer for the waiting couple. "You leave me no choice then," Pete says after the woman tells Greg it's her first married Christmas and the snow deer will look charming in their home. "You *have* to play Santa for me," Pete insists as soon as the couple turns to leave.

"What? No way. Where's Wes?" Greg asks, scanning the crowd of people. "He can do it."

"He and Jane are on their way to the fire department's ugly sweater Christmas party," Pete says with a glance at his watch.

"Swell." Greg straightens a fallen deer in the booth display. "But don't look at me, Dad. Find someone else."

"Son," Pete says. Then nothing. Nothing until Greg looks over at him. "I really *need* you to do it," Pete adds while lifting a whittled stag. "Buck up!"

"Fine, then. Fine. Can't be any worse than what I went through last night."

With that, Greg snatches up a box holding the Santa costume before skulking out behind the Near and Deer booth. Looking both ways to be sure no one's watching, he pulls out the Santa pants and begrudgingly steps into them.

There's a loud zip sound as Pete cracks open the back wall of the booth tent.

"Hey! Some privacy, please!" Greg quietly yells.

166

"But I meant to ask you," Pete says. "How *did* it go at that auction thing last night?"

"Not good."

"And I'm not surprised. With those whiskers, it's obvious you haven't shaved in days."

Greg looks at his father as he hikes the Santa pants around his waist. "This is the *new* Greg Davis, Dad. How many times do I have to tell you?" Greg reaches for the red velvet, fur-trimmed Santa coat and puts it on over his stuffed Santa belly.

"Keep that look up," Pete warns with his head poked through the partially unzipped canvas tent-back, "and you won't be *needing* the Santa beard. So who's your date this year?"

"Don't ask."

"Come on. It can't be that bad."

"I don't want to talk about it." Buckling the costume's wide shiny black belt, Greg glares at his father. "That date can't be done and over with soon enough."

"Spill it already."

Greg's quiet for a moment as he loops the elastic straps of a long white beard and wig around his ears. "Lindsey Haynes," he finally admits.

"What?" Instantly there's a loud *ziiiip* sound as Pete completely opens the rear wall of the tent and steps out. "*Gus'* niece? Isn't she the lady who backed her house into your car?"

"She is." Bent over while taking off his shoes and putting on shiny black boots with a white fur cuff, Greg glances up at his father. "The one and only."

"Now that's not *so* bad, son. She's about your age, and very pretty. Nice, too."

"Pretty and nice got me nowhere the past three Christmases, Dad. Vera, Jane and Penny. All three? Pretty and nice—and each one left me with a broken heart."

"Listen. I'm getting a real frosty vibe outta you this year. And it's needless. I met that Lindsey the other day. She placed a custom whittled deer order, special for her parents. Real sweet, she is. When I mentioned you were my boy, she said that you two keep bumping into each other. Matter of fact ..." Pete steps closer and lowers his voice. "She's picking up her order on her dinner break. Any minute now."

Greg's already walking toward the North Pole Station and its waiting green chair. "And don't you go bringing up the whole date thing," he calls back as he pulls on his red velvet stocking cap, then pulls the pom-pom tip over his shoulder. "Don't be meddling!"

⁂

Lindsey doesn't mind eating her dinner outside The Main Course booth at the Merry Market. George, the deli's owner, set out bistro tables around a roaring firepit, so it's warm enough to linger there. Seeing the flames flicker and spark to the sky, and hearing other patrons chatting all around her, it could feel like she's at an intimate holiday dinner. When a server brings out her order of hot soup and a half sandwich, Lindsey recognizes her as Amy, from the historical society's auction the night before.

"Don't you own Wedding Wishes?" Lindsey asks as Amy sets down the food tray.

"I do! Is there a wedding in your future?" Amy asks back with a friendly wink.

"No, I own a vintage clothing boutique, and saw your gown last night at the auction. It would've been perfect for my inventory, so I was hoping to bid on it. But I was late arriving."

"Oh … Well, stop by my shop and have a look at the clearance rack. There are a few real bargains there."

"Any winter gowns?"

Amy nods, then turns to pick up another customer's order. "One with matching long velvet gloves," she says over her shoulder.

Lindsey waves goodbye, and after her last sip of hot soup, she wanders to Near and Deer's booth. Her custom order should be ready by now. As she approaches, she recognizes someone. Recognizes a familiar tweed newsboy cap on top of a white head of hair. Recognizes a familiar face, too, one with twinkling eyes.

"Uncle Gus!" she calls out, then gives him a quick hug.

"Lindsey." He looks past her to her tiny house parked on the far side of The Green. "Shouldn't you be manning your store?"

"Dinner break," she assures him. "I close up for an hour or so."

"I've got your order all ready," Pete says, reaching for a box on his booth floor.

"And I'm just leaving," Gus remarks, patting Lindsey's arm. "Time for my night shift driving the Holly Trolley."

"Have fun, Uncle Gus," she tells him.

"And Pete," Gus adds. "Don't forget tomorrow."

"I won't," Pete says while setting Lindsey's box on his booth counter. "Pizza at Luigi's?"

"About six." Gus tips his hat in a casual farewell while walking away. "I'll save us a booth," he calls back.

Lindsey waves to him, then turns to Pete as he puts her deer order in a shopping bag. She steps closer, quietly asking, "Is Greg around?"

"My son? You just missed him."

"I did? Darn, I had something to ask him about what time … Tuesday … It's just that … Oh, never mind." She gives him a quick, apologetic smile.

"No worries, Lindsey. I mean, Greg's *here*, just not here with me," Pete explains. "He's over at the North Pole Station, filling in as Santa this evening."

Lindsey can't help it then, the way she whips around and spots a Santa Claus talking to kids on his lap—a Santa with a blue-eyed twinkle. Which makes her spin right back around to Pete, hike her purse up on her shoulder, glance over her shoulder again and adjust her slouchy beanie, then start to leave. "Okay, Pete. Well, thank you! It was nice chatting."

In a moment, Pete's voice calls to her. "Lindsey! Wait!"

She turns back with a small smile, wondering what he might want.

Quirking an eyebrow, Pete lifts a shopping bag by its handles and holds it up high. "You forgot your custom deer."

seventeen

JOLLY JIMINY! IT CAN'T BE so. Lindsey glances back over her shoulder, but there's no denying it. Does she really have a crush ... on *Santa*?

On a certain tall, blue-eyed Santa? One whose scruff of whiskers shows above his cottony white beard?

Why else would the sight of him have her hightail it back to her tiny house without remembering to take her package from Pete at Near and Deer?

Swell, she thinks. Now even Pete saw her festively flustered.

Making her way through the after-dinner crowd of shoppers, Lindsey squeezes around folks browsing the tents; passes families eating warm salted pretzels; hurries by elves holding trays of free candy canes. All she wants to do is get back to her shop and get busy selling her wares.

Until, for the second time in five minutes, she hears someone call out her name.

172

"Lindsey!"

When she turns while holding her large shopping bag, it's to see another familiar, friendly face.

"Need help with your parcel?" he asks, then bites into one of those free candy canes.

Lindsey squints at the man wearing a gray down jacket, unzipped, over a plaid shirt and corduroy pants. "Oh, umm … Brian from the post office, right?" she asks. "Nice to see you again."

"We keep running into each other around here."

"We do! How are you?" Lindsey asks, glad for the distraction from, well, from Santa.

"I'm good, Lindsey. How about you?" He motions to her Near and Deer shopping bag. "Doing some shopping?"

"Oh, this?" She raises her bag and shrugs. "A little. But mostly I'm working. Heading back to my shop now." As she says it, she turns and points in its direction. "Vagabond Vintage."

"In the tiny house everyone's talking about?" Brian steps closer and looks past her to the shingled dwelling. "That's *your* shop?"

"It is. I travel from place to place and sell vintage clothing, accessories. Some things for the home, too."

"Wow, that's awesome. Hey, listen. My wife *loves* vintage things and was telling me she heard about this shop on wheels," Brian says as he finishes his candy cane. "Maybe you can help me pick out something for her? Something nice for Christmas?"

"I'd be glad to, Brian."

He checks his watch. "Okay, great. But I'm actually on my way out now. How about if I swing by sometime next week?"

"Perfect." Lindsey backs up in the direction of her shop. "I'll be here in the afternoons."

"Okay, then. I'll stop in," Brian says, giving a small wave while turning to leave. But he turns back once more. "Hope you're enjoying the holiday season," he tells her, stepping forward to shake her hand—a gesture that somehow turns into an awkward hug.

Lindsey hugs him back, patting his shoulder with a laugh before she pulls away, smiles and returns to her shop, pronto.

◦◦◦

By early evening, twinkling Christmas lights transform The Green. The way they illuminate rosy-cheeked faces, and light up the tall town tree, and wrap around colonial-style lampposts ... the scene looks straight out of those holiday movies Greg likes to watch. Tonight, he could practically have the starring role in one as he sits in an overstuffed green velvet chair and plays Santa to Addison's children.

After bending low to hear the Christmas wishes of a boy of about five, Greg hands him off to an assistant elf. Saying, "Ho! Ho! Ho!" he looks to see who's next in line, but someone else catches Greg's eye. There's no mistaking that it's ... Lindsey Haynes. She's holding a large shopping bag while crossing The Green. He can't miss that long blonde hair beneath her slouchy beanie. Just then, she turns to talk to someone—and she's all friendly smiles, chatting animatedly, then pointing to her tiny house.

So Greg leans forward and squints through the glow of Christmas lights. Wait. He actually recognizes the person talking to Lindsey. It's the same man from the tree lot at Cooper Hardware.

All right, then. Maybe she *was* telling the truth yesterday when she said her date-bid was accidental. Because from the looks of her happy face, she's smitten with this guy. She could even be dating *him*, this … this … *Brian*. Yeah, that was his name.

Greg's certain of it now—that they're a couple—when he gives one more look. Right then, Brian is laughing and moving close to Lindsey, before reaching his arms around her in a hug. When they pull apart, Lindsey is still smiling as she backs away and waves goodbye.

So. There you go.

It's why Greg stopped trying this year. And rightly so. Because the old Greg Davis would have *utterly* deflated upon seeing Lindsey in that holiday hug.

But not the new Greg. The new, assuredly unattached and heart-safe Greg Davis shrugs his Santa-suit-clad shoulders and moves on.

"Ho! Ho! Ho!" he booms to the boy sitting on his lap. "You look very familiar. What's your name now?" he asks, bending low to listen to the shy boy who's got earmuffs on his head.

175

"Owen," the boy quietly answers while looking cautiously up at Greg's Santa face.

"Owen! I know your mom and dad. They always put in a good word for you at the North Pole." Greg looks out to the crowd and waves to Sara Beth Riley standing close by, taking a picture of her son sitting with Santa.

"Now what would you like for Christmas, Owen?" Greg asks.

It's a question he asks the next tot, and the next, and the next. The odd thing is that he suddenly doesn't mind this Santa duty. Even though it'll be a busy night, with that line of kids wrapping halfway around The Green, Greg's feeling unexpectedly relieved. If Lindsey has somebody in her life, it means there will be no awkward tension on their auction date Tuesday night. No stress. No romantic pinings. She's already spoken for by this Brian guy. Her smiles and hug said it all.

Still. As the children keep coming—some with a gentle nudge from a parent, some with eyes sparkling with delight, some Santa-awestruck into silence—and as secret Christmas wishes are all revealed to him when he tips down his beard-covered face, Greg can't seem to look away from that one tiny house in the distance. Between each child sitting on his lap, and tugging on his beard, and telling their own personal Christmas wish, he steals a furtive glance.

All while his *Ho! Ho! Ho!* is somehow dialed down a notch.

Once back in her shop, Lindsey gets down to business. Being busy is one way to stop wondering if—*seriously?*—she has a *crush* on the temperamental doctor she backed her house into.

"Oh, nonsense," she whispers while setting her old-world Santa beside a small velvet display case of cameo pendants, filigree rings and silver bracelets. "Crushing on Santa!" she exclaims as she glances out the window in the direction of the North Pole Station.

A kiss will tell all, Lindsey remembers Penny saying this morning. *A kiss will tell all.*

"Well, by gosh, by golly, I'm going to walk over to Greg and try to find out … *something!*"

But when she glances out her tiny house window again, customers are passing the OPEN sign she'd flipped back after her dinner break, and they're all coming right up her steps to browse Vagabond Vintage.

One thing Lindsey notices is this: The closer it gets to Christmas, the more intent the shoppers. They've got lists clutched in gloved hands as they push into the shop. Hangers are swept side to side; countertop boxes are rummaged through.

Still, her mind is made up. She has to get over to that North Pole Station before Greg's Santa shift ends. As she rings out people, and wraps a silver spoon bracelet in tissue, she steals glances outside her window. *With one kiss,* Lindsey wonders, *will I know for certain?*

Once her customers have left, she glances out onto The Green again. Booths are strung with twinkling lights;

the town tree soars, all aglow, in the center of everything; a sea of wool caps and beanies atop parkas and peacoats meanders from booth to firepit to food truck.

But there, in one area, the line is getting shorter—the line of people waiting to talk to Santa.

So Lindsey does it.

She closes up shop, puts on her shearling-trimmed suede coat and slouchy beanie, and heads out. But not without first stopping and giving her snowman snow globe a shake so that her heart will know what to do.

Then she walks across The Green. The air is cold, the crowd thinning as evening settles in. She passes a booth selling Town of Addison sweatshirts and caps; hurries by Circa 1765's booth selling small mantel clocks and antique picture frames. With each step, she's closer to finding out if Penny's advice will work.

"But I can't very well kiss Santa in front of everyone," she whispers to herself as she stops in her tracks and spins around to head back to her tiny house. So her plan will never work.

Unless, she thinks with a glance back over her shoulder. Unless she simply tells Santa her secret Christmas wish ... to give fate a little nudge! Of course! Getting herself to the end of the line, her plan comes together as she summons every ounce of Christmas courage. But for this to work, she can't let on that she knows Santa is actually Greg.

Velvet ropes looped to brass posts block off the big green chair from the Santa line. Amy from the bridal shop

stands beside Santa's chair now. Her little daughter—
Grace, Lindsey overhears—sits on Santa's knee and looks
up at his face while touching his white beard. Greg talks
to the child, then leans low to hear her Christmas wish.
Finally Amy lifts her daughter off his lap and takes a candy
cane from Santa's elf-assistant.

"Next!" the elf calls out. He's dressed in green velvet,
with a jingle-bell collar and striped stockings, his shoes
curling at the toe. "Do you have a little one?" he asks
Lindsey.

"Umm." Lindsey takes a tentative step closer. "Well,
no."

Which gets the elf to turn up his hands, exasperated.

Which gets Lindsey a bit desperate. "But I *do* have a
special request for Santa?" With her question, she shakes
off her jolly jitters. "Would that be okay?"

"I guess so." The elf nods her way. "Sure, why not?
Santa's team is very accommodating."

Lindsey hesitates, clutching her mittened hands
together, until the busy elf motions her to advance
beyond the velvet rope barrier, straight to Santa's chair.

⚬⚬⚬

Greg's finally got the knack of this Santa gig. It's actually
fun, if he had to say so. Giving another big wave to little
Grace with her mother, he's feeling pretty charitable—
hearing the children's Christmas wishes and sending them
off with holiday hope. That was the one piece of advice

his father gave him when he was putting on the Santa costume.

Ask to hear a secret wish of what they want for Christmas, Pete had said. *Everybody loves to share a secret!*

So it's with a relaxed "*Ho! Ho! Ho!*" that he turns to see who's next in line.

A *Ho! Ho! Ho!* that he stifles when he sees Lindsey Haynes approaching. Surely she doesn't know that it's him beneath that white beard and wig. And heck, his padded stomach looks so realistic, she'd never figure out his identity. So he clears his throat, somewhat changes his voice and tries again.

"*Ho! Ho! Ho!*" he repeats. "And what brings you to Santa, young lady?"

Lindsey takes a cautious step, looks back at the elf-assistant, then takes another step. "Um, Santa?" she asks.

"Come closer." Feeling well concealed in his red velvet Santa costume, Greg waves her over.

Lindsey doesn't say anything. She just stops and looks over her shoulder again.

"There's room for two here." Greg moves over in his large green chair. "Something you want to ask Santa Claus? I'm taking lots of wish requests today."

"Well, there is *one* little thing."

"Christmas wishes do come true. But hey," he says, leaning toward her. "You look a little sad. Let's see if I can grant your wish and get that smile back."

"Maybe this is wrong." Lindsey shakes her head and stops again.

180

"No, no," Greg insists in a deeper-than-usual voice while extending his velvet-sleeved arm to her. From beneath his sleeve's white fur cuff, he stretches out his gloved hand.

Wordlessly, Lindsey steps closer and takes his hand. "Santa, I don't want anyone to overhear."

Okay, well now that she's this close, a new round of perspiration beads across Greg's forehead. This near to him, might she decipher who he really is? He pushes up his bushy white beard, clears his throat again and pats the chair seat.

But it's when he slides over in the stuffed velvet, extra-wide chair that the surprise hits him. It happens so gosh darn suddenly, he doesn't even know how to react. Lindsey rushes over faster than a flying reindeer, squeezes in the chair beside him, cups her mouth and presses it to his ear.

"If you can make only *one* of my wishes come true," she whispers, her breath warm against his ear. "Let it be this …"

In her pause, Greg leans even closer. His skin is now clammy beneath his velvet-and-fur-laden costume. If she knew it was him sitting there, would she even have approached Santa this evening? Already she's anxious about it. He can tell by her iron grip on his velvet-sleeved arm when she presses her soft mouth against his ear to reveal her wish.

Again, Lindsey whispers close. "From a certain sweet guy, one special kiss … this Christmas."

181

As soon as her last word leaves her lips, she bolts—just like that! Just jumps up and runs off like the prettiest doe through the woods.

"*Wait!*" Greg shouts as he stands, too.

Whether she hears him or not, he'll never know. Lindsey Haynes just keeps running, her blonde hair flying behind her, her slouchy hat slipping off so that she stops to scoop it up. Then she runs again—pushing this way around an idled couple, that way past an elf handing out red-and-white striped candy canes.

Greg watches her, then looks to two children waiting in line with his elf-assistant now. So Greg slowly sinks back down in his green velvet chair, whispering, "*A kiss?*"

Again he looks out onto The Green as Lindsey gets smaller and smaller in the distance. Twinkling lights strung on the booths, and around the tall town Christmas tree, give a misty look to the sight before him. For a moment longer he watches her flee to her tiny house. And the whole time he watches, it's with one singular, specific thought in mind.

A *kiss?* From who? From that Brian guy she was hugging moments ago? They looked seriously friendly, from Greg's vantage point in his enormous green velvet Santa chair.

Or did she mean a kiss, he wonders, *from me?*

eighteen

THE THING IS, IT DOESN'T matter. None of it.

Doesn't matter whose kiss Lindsey wishes for. Doesn't matter if *he's* the sweet guy she meant, or if Brian is. What difference does it make, anyway? Sometimes Greg has to remind himself that it's for precisely this tormented reason that he's sitting out the game of love this holiday season. Watching from the bench as potential dates and dalliances pass him right by.

Because they always end up in heartbreak. Or annoyance—as some other dude sweeps in and steals the girl. A few laughs at a wedding reception three years ago, and Vera Sterling looked his way—until Derek Cooper delighted her. And after a hay-bale dance with Jane March at Coveside Cornucopia a couple years past? His own woebegone brother, Wes, won her over.

Then last year was the last straw, when Greg came *so* close. Things were warming up between Penny Hart and himself as he tended to her injured arm, *and* brought her a special care package out at Cardinal Cabin—with the hopes of sharing the wine and popcorn and holiday movies in that basket. Until a certain part-time lumberjack looked her way, and Frank Lombardo got the girl.

So now, after working a long and full Sunday shift at the hospital, Greg's tired and has only one thought on the Lindsey Haynes Christmas wish matter: Kiss ... *schmiss*. There hasn't been time to even stock up on groceries lately, never mind ruminate on romance. Reason enough, after clocking out at work, to stop in at Luigi's Pizza for dinner, alone.

Sitting in a booth against the side wall, he digs into the Sunday Special—sausage and peppers over pasta. There's something to be said for eating alone, anyway. He did enough talking and thinking all day at the hospital. At last, he can quietly unwind. So after sprinkling a hefty amount of Parmesan over his meal, he leans over the plate and simply forks in a hunk of the saucy-peppery mishmash. Around him, gold tinsel garland drapes across the ceiling, with red glitter bells angled in each loop. On the wall beside his booth, a framed still life of Tuscan tables set with wine bottles, cheese and grapes is outlined in colored twinkly lights. Other patrons—a few young couples, a family with kids—chatter at nearby tables. Greg takes it all in while raising his pasta-laden, sauce-dripping fork.

This is actually the best meal he's had in days.

Until the door opens and he gives a quick glance over at his father, Pete, entering Luigi's with his old friend, Gus.

"Swell," Greg whispers while sinking down in his booth seat. He's beat, it's been a long day, and he doesn't really feel like company. The two men approach from behind and—wouldn't you know it—sit in the empty booth right before his. At least they didn't recognize him from that angle, probably because they're too busy talking town gossip already.

At the very least, thank goodness for tall booth backs. Now if Greg can just finish his meal in peace, he'll say hello on his way out. With his father and Gus settled in the booth behind him—coats off, hats set aside, pizza ordered—Greg slinks lower and keeps eating. He takes one mouthful of the cheesy, saucy concoction, then another. But after the third fork-lift, he stops—mid-chew.

What? Greg tips his head slightly, listening to his father and Gus go at it behind him. *I'm their topic of conversation?*

"That boy of yours," Gus is saying. "Not behaving like he used to."

"Which one?" Pete asks.

"The good doctor. Greg. Got a real attitude going on, and that car! Doesn't seem like the old Greg Davis I used to know."

"It's not," Pete assures him. "He told me he's employing a different strategy to get through the holidays this year." Pete lowers his voice. "*Alone*," he harshly whispers. "I'll tell you something, Gus. My son's putting up a hard shell, is what he's doing. Last few years, he got burned. Found some lovely ladies he was interested in here in town, and now they're all spoken for."

"Funny you should mention that. I used to see Greg out at Cardinal Cabin visiting Penny Hart last December," Gus says around a mouthful of some overloaded pizza their waitress delivered. "Sometimes they'd walk together around the lake."

Greg waits silently while Gus gulps his soda, then sets down his glass. "But she'd walk with that *Frank*, too."

"Yup," Pete explains. "That's why my boy says he has a new attitude this year. Got burned one too many times. So I'm not sure that it's really an *attitude* he's got, or if he's still licking his wounds. Can't seem to find a doe of his own."

"I don't know about that, Pete." The clatter of silverware clicks on a plate as Gus puts in more of his two cents' worth—apparently while digging into a salad now. "Something there between your son and my niece maybe?"

"Lindsey?"

"Why, yes. You know ..." Gus adds, lowering *his* voice now, "I even tried to set them up a bit. Gave Greg a line of malarkey about my rotator cuff and got him to stop by the cabin to check it out." More fork-salad spearing, then, "Had him over at dinnertime. With Lindsey there, too ... if you get my drift."

"Hot dog! Maybe it worked. Because I talked to Lindsey at the Merry Market. At the mere mention of Greg, I noticed her rosy cheeks. So ... was she just cold, or was she blushing?"

"Okay. So Greg being gruff might just be a big *bluff*, my friend."

"Oh, but wait! You haven't heard the latest, Gus."

"What's that?"

"Lindsey bid on a date with Greg at that historical society auction. She placed the *highest* bid, actually. They're going out Tuesday."

"Is that right?" Gus asks, chowing into another pizza slice. "Hey, I've got an idea. It's my shift driving the Holly Trolley Tuesday. I'll clear it out, and if we can get those two on it, they'll have the trolley all to themselves. I'll give them a nice romantic tour through town, stop on the covered bridge. It worked for Penny and Frank last year, could work again ..."

"Maybe," Pete agrees. "But one date Tuesday, then what?"

"Good question. What can we do to get them together again?"

Greg abruptly stands and turns to them. "Nothing," he insists to their collective gasp—which buys him a second to scoop up the last of his sausage and peppers. "You'll do absolutely *nothing*," he says around his mouthful of food before tossing down his fork.

"Son!" Pete exclaims, turning in his padded booth to see Greg. "You've been sitting there this whole time?"

Greg, still chewing the last of his saucy peppers, lifts his leather bomber from his booth seat and slips it on. "Yep," he answers while walking to Pete's booth. "And that's about *enough* out of you two," he almost yells while slamming his fist on the table between the two men. "Enough!"

"Careful, son," Pete warns him. "Your hand."

Greg glances at the other customers—some sending worried glances his way—then lowers his voice. "After my date with Lindsey—a *purchased* date, if I may remind you—there will be nothing more. No trolley rides," he growls at Gus. "No holiday hijinks or merry matchmaking out of you two busybodies."

"But—" Gus starts.

"Nope," Greg cuts him off. "Nothing," he says while pulling his wallet from his pocket and slipping out enough cash to cover his bill. "You two should be *ashamed* of yourselves, meddling in the affairs of others," he adds while dropping his money on his own table. "And Lindsey's seeing someone, anyway." That line's tossed in for good measure, or for shock value, or ... *whatever*, he thinks as he zips his leather bomber and hikes up the collar. "Saw them together outside her shop yesterday," Greg throws back at them before heading to the exit.

"Son!" Pete calls. From the sound of his voice, he must've half stood with insistence. "So you *do* care!" his father's voice echoes across the busy restaurant.

Greg does nothing but wave him off. "Eh," he says, pushing open the door to the cold December night.

nineteen

BY TUESDAY EVENING, LINDSEY HAS stopped regretting her impulsive, mistaken wedding-gown bid—one that instead secured her a date with Greg Davis. It's quiet, here at Snowflake Lake. And that silence leaves plenty of room for now *hopeful* thoughts. Standing in a turtleneck sweater dress in front of the mirror, she loops a wide belt low on her hips and scans her reflection. From the top of her straight blonde hair to the boots on her feet, everything is just right for their date: her bangs wispy, the plum-colored dress fitted, the boots knee-high over black tights.

"Maybe tonight … a kiss will reveal all," she says to her old-world Santa standing near the doorway.

When the unmistakable rumble of a Mustang Fastback grows close, she peeks out the window. Greg is walking along the stone path between the two tall pine trees. He's got on his leather bomber over a sweater and dark pants. She opens the door for him and is surprised when he

189

holds out a corsage box from Fancy Florals.

"That's so nice of you," Lindsey says as he steps into her tiny house.

"It was provided," he admits while pulling off his gloves. "You know, by the historical society. But, well …" He sets his gloves on her fold-down table. "Here, I'll put it on." He lifts out the wrist corsage of tiny cream-color dried flowers and two mini-pinecones set in greens. A few pearl beads dot the arrangement. "Are you a leftie? Or rightie?" he asks.

"Rightie."

"Okay, so it won't get in the way of your eating, I'll put it on your left."

Lindsey silently nods, folds back the sleeve of her sweater dress and extends her arm. It surprises her when his fingers tremble as he stretches the corsage's elastic and slips it over her fingers, to her wrist. With his recent brusque attitude, she'd thought he'd be more cool, calm and collected. He then twists the corsage to straighten it, all while clearing his throat before gently releasing her hand and stepping back.

"Okay, then," he says, watching her closely.

"Thank you," Lindsey whispers before lifting a shawl off the table bench. "We should go?"

When Greg nods, she wraps her gray-plaid, thickly fringed shawl around her shoulders, then is surprised yet again.

"You look pretty tonight," Greg tells her. "I mean, you always look pretty. But …"

Lindsey reaches for her purse on the table. "Well, it is a date after all!" she says while motioning him to the door, which she locks up before stepping out into the dark night. Walking over the stone pathway to Greg's car, she can't help but notice one nearby cabin's illuminated front window, where one heavyset man with white hair is wearing a cardigan and lifting the curtain by a familiar puzzle table. Tuesday nights are Gus' Holly Trolley night shifts, but it's early still, and he must not have left yet. Lindsey sneaks a wave to her uncle, who waves right back—with a requisite twinkle in his eye, too.

And so, much as she'd thought it would, her purchased date begins.

⌒≈◯

As they make small talk in the dark car headed to Cedar Ridge Tavern, Lindsey notices a change from Greg's tentative tenderness in her tiny house. Driving past shopfronts outlined in white lights now, and cruising by garland-wrapped lampposts, the closer they get to their date destination, the more withdrawn he becomes. It's obvious in the sometimes-quiet car that he still hasn't warmed up to this date idea. He seemed to dread it from the get-go—starting at the hospital's holiday party at the Addison Boathouse, when women there teased him about it—to right now, actually living the date.

"Why don't you park around back, and be discreet?" Lindsey suggests as they arrive at the restaurant. Throngs of local news reporters and photographers wait huddled in their coats and scarves—cameras in hand. "We'll duck in and out, and be done in no time."

Greg throws her a quick glance. "Oh, Miss Haynes. That is *not* how this works." He downshifts and his black car rumbles into a special parking space. Velvet ropes line each side of the space; a RESERVED sign is in front of it; and—unbelievably—a red carpet leads from their parking space to the restaurant's front entrance.

"Wait right there," Greg tells her when he shuts off the car and the cameras begin flashing.

What Lindsey sees by his getting out—by his rushing around and opening her door, then giving her his arm to escort her inside the restaurant—is this: Greg knows the auctioned-date routine. He's been there, done that, and is quickly going through the motions again, tonight. Anything, it seems, to just get through this.

Which leaves her wondering if they'll even come *close* to a kiss—a little one, at the very least. Still, she holds his leather-bomber-clad arm and leans into him as those camera flashes light up here, and there, and over thataway—not letting up until Greg walks her inside, beneath swags of green garland, to the dimly lit, hushed restaurant.

"Dinner for two," Greg finally tells a woman standing at the hostess station in the lobby.

"Yes, of course! We've been *waiting* for you," she exclaims, scooping up two menus. She takes their coats first, then leads them past a bar with amber lights hanging over it, and with tabletop Christmas trees illuminating either end. Beyond the bar, they enter the dining room and pass candlelit tables, then walk beside a half-wall, straight to a tiny round table beside a roaring stone fireplace.

As soon as Greg pulls out Lindsey's chair, the Roving Reporter from the *Addison Weekly* rushes over. "Just have a few questions, folks. Then I'll be out of your way and you can enjoy your evening."

Lindsey sits, puts down her purse and straightens her sweater dress. All the while, the reporter pulls up a chair, and a waitress pours two complimentary glasses of champagne before setting the bottle in an ice bucket. Meanwhile, that reporter is scooting his chair closer to the table and taking out his pad and pen.

All this attention is surprising, actually, enough so that Lindsey's bewildered by the commotion—by the fluttering activity every which way she turns: camera flashes and an insistent hostess and reporters and onlookers. By the time she takes it all in and catches Greg's eye, he simply raises his champagne glass and touches it to hers.

"Cheers," he says with a small nod.

And so she does the same, whispering "Cheers," before sipping her drink.

"Three quick questions for you two lovebirds," the reporter begins.

Lovebirds. *If only*, Lindsey thinks.

Wait. Scratch that. If only a *kiss*, that would be enough.

Because one little kiss, and according to Penny, she'll know.

Annoyance? Or a spark.

Meanwhile, the reporter taps his pen point on his pad. "Question one." At their almost-too-small candlelit table, he looks from Greg, to Lindsey. "Any romance in the air tonight?"

Lindsey jumps right in, much, she supposes, to Greg's relief. "Oh, I'll take this one," she answers. "Love is *always* around us. I own a vintage clothing shop and come across many dusty finds. What I've learned is that when you simply brush the dust off things ..." She glances to Greg with a small smile, then gets back to her answer. "Brush the dust off ... *moments*, even," she nearly whispers, thinking of the *moment* her tiny house backed into Greg Davis' luxury sedan, "there's often a treasure beneath it all."

With his pen scratching across his notepad, the reporter fires off his second question. "Have to ask this one, it's the talk of the town." He dots an i and looks out at the crowded restaurant, then at Greg and Lindsey. "What do you think of Addison's new traffic roundabout?"

Lindsey's sigh must almost be palpable. Her sigh of *relief*. Talk of the town? She'd thought, surely, that question would be about her purchased date, and the intent of her high bid.

"Keeps driving interesting," Greg is saying instead. "Stop, go. Hesitate, merge. And those blaring horns. You never know *what* situation you'll find in that traffic circle."

"Final question." The reporter jots it on his pad as he

194

asks, "Tell me. Readers will hang on your *every* word. What do you want for Christmas this year?"

"Oh!" Lindsey begins with a guarded smile. "I *cannot* tell!"

Raising an eyebrow, the reporter looks at her.

"No, because you see …" she says, leaning close to him. "Christmas wishes are *thee* very best. But *my* Christmas wish is personal … just between me and Santa," she says with a slight glance at Greg—who is sitting back, arms crossed, and watching her with some amusement. Lindsey leans even closer to the reporter and clasps his arm, saying, "I already told Santa what I want for Christmas on The Green."

❧

As Greg sits back in his chair; as he draws his hand across his three-days-unshaven face; as the flames snap and pop in the fireplace beside their table; as he finally leans forward and waves off the Roving Reporter; as he orders chicken parmigiana and Lindsey orders pasta primavera; as their knees bump beneath the tiny table; as their wineglasses are refilled and candlelight flickers, he cannot get one darn question out of his head.

The thought has been lodged there—stuck solidly—since Lindsey squeezed beside him in the green velvet Santa chair Saturday night, leaned close, pressed her mouth to his ear and shared her Christmas wish: *From a certain sweet guy, one special kiss … this Christmas.*

195

But the question is … From *which* guy?

As their tiramisu and raspberry-drizzled cheesecake desserts are devoured; as Lindsey's bangs brush her brown eyes—eyes that sparkle in the candlelight; as their talk wanders from family, to work, to hidden hobbies—his ballroom dancing, hers chocolate-chip cookie baking; as he laughs at something she says and she squeezes his arm in return, something *else* happens while he still ponders that one, pivotal question.

What happens is this: They lean closer over the table. Their hands brush. They actually sample each other's dessert. A second hand-bump happens as they both reach for the coffee creamer—except this time, they don't jolt back.

That's when Lindsey—Lindsey Haynes with the pretty eyes and soft hair, Lindsey wearing a plum-colored dress with a silver pendant—does it. Yes, she gives him the opportunity he's been waiting for.

Gives him the chance to get an answer to his kiss conundrum.

"So," she quietly asks while leaning close across the table, "you *really* don't have a girlfriend?"

Greg shakes his head and rubs his whiskered jaw as he considers his answer. "This here," he says, motioning his hand between them. "This here is my *only* date of the season." He sits closer, then, too. "And how about you?"

"What about me?" she asks back, her eyes smiling, her earrings glimmering in the candlelight.

Greg pauses. This is it. The kiss-question lodged in his head will finally be answered. Once and for all. *Who does she want a Christmas kiss from?* Brian, or him? Right now, he'll know. "So. Well, are you seeing—"

"Dr. *Davis*! Miss *Haynes*!" their breathless hostess says as she rushes to their table. Lindsey's gray-plaid shawl and Greg's leather bomber are in her hands. "Your horse-and-buggy ride *awaits*," she declares while distributing his jacket and Lindsey's shawl.

That's all it takes. Yes, the night changes then. As they're whisked through the dark restaurant out to the cold air and the waiting horse-drawn carriage, passing photographers' flashing cameras, Greg's burning question is left hanging over the winter night.

Lindsey's Christmas wish whispered to Santa, a whispered wish about a mystery kiss … is now a thought he'll just have to dismiss.

twenty

LINDSEY THINKS SHE'S NEVER LANDED in a town so charming. Of course, it helps that she's seeing it tonight from a padded carriage bench, that carriage being led by a prancing horse. From her vantage point, Addison looks like a ceramic Christmas village come to life: saltbox colonials and Cape Cod homes; candlelit windows; twinkly lights and cottony snow tucked in shop display windows; a white-steepled chapel and white picket fences; carolers; the clip-clop of horse hooves through the covered bridge.

It's no surprise that Lindsey finds herself falling for this magical town.

And maybe falling for a certain someone, too.

Tonight's a night seeming straight out of a storybook. Everything—the pretty streets, the date, even the jingling bells slung over the horse's shoulders—has Lindsey feel that all the Christmas stars are aligned above her.

Their driver, Derek Cooper, finally steers the carriage

toward Addison Cove. On its banks, Snowflakes and Coffee Cakes' Christmas barn is illuminated, and busy! Shoppers rush past the two twinkling fir trees outside its red-painted door. Lindsey's view gets even better once the carriage turns into the cove parking lot. The waterside scene is so wondrous—even the dock pilings are strung in swags of white lights.

As though straight out of another century, Derek stops the carriage and ties the horse to an actual stone hitching post, a lone remnant here from a bygone time.

"You've got a few minutes, kids," he says while giving the horse's neck a pat.

"What?" Greg asks from the carriage seat. "Wait."

"I'm going over to see Vera, grab myself a pastry from Snowflakes and Coffee Cakes." Derek walks backward in the big barn's direction. "Vera keeps the shop open late during the holidays. So hey, give a whistle when you're ready to take off," he adds, slowly trotting up the banks of the cove to the imposing brown barn.

Which effectively leaves Lindsey and Greg utterly alone, in a horse-drawn carriage, at the gently lapping water's edge.

Lindsey looks out at the cove. Moonlight dapples the water ripples, and at the far end, a stand of trees rises in silhouette in the night. But it's when she looks over to the illuminated Christmas barn with its tiny lights, and candlelit windows casting a glow on holiday figurines, and ornament displays, and genuine ceramic villages inside, that it happens.

She knows now. Yes, it's one week until Christmas … and her kiss-wish might be about to come true.

⌒♥◯

If ever Greg's felt panic, it's now.

He's immersed in a situation that can take his holiday right down. Because, so far, his heart's been intact this holiday season. A little steely, maybe … but, well, steely's suited him this year.

Actually, steely is helping him reach his goal: make it through Christmas with no disappointment, no love lost, no hurt heart. Just a few weeks ago, it's why he threw three darts at Joel's Bar and Grille—one dart zinged for each love he *did* lose during the past three holiday seasons.

Yes, three strikes and he's out. Thinking of throwing those darts reminds him that he's sitting out this season on the bench.

The problem is the picturesque view before him. Tonight the cove water glimmers with starlight. The Christmas barn on its banks is aglow with candles and twinkly lights. It's all taunting him, these evocative sights, tempting him to get back in the game!

He glances at the beautiful woman beside him in the horse-drawn carriage. Lindsey sits there, and he just knows she's waiting for her one Christmas wish to be granted.

But … but, but, but. This night's not *real*. Every minute of it's been set up, and is therefore fake. He's not denying that this date's been sweet, but he's also not denying that it was organized to romantic perfection by any vendor who donated to the historical society's auction. Cooper Hardware? The carriage ride. Cedar Ridge Tavern? The dinner. Fancy Florals? The corsage.

One thing's for certain: The old Greg Davis would've been *all* over this. The romantic evening outings, the sweet talk? It's straight out of his old rule book.

So it's really important to remember that *this* is when it all turns. Oh, yeah. You *think* you've got romance in the palm of your hand when suddenly … oh, the letdown is too familiar to Greg.

"What a nice night," Lindsey says, interrupting his pathetic inner monologue. "It isn't what I'd expected it to be."

"Nothing ever is."

Lindsey shivers beside him, so Greg pulls the carriage blanket over her lap. It doesn't seem enough, though, so he gives her his burgundy scarf, too—gently looping it around her neck and shoulders.

"Better?" Greg asks.

The moment is quiet. Water laps lightly at shore when Lindsey touches his face and whispers, "Much better."

Greg's eyes don't leave hers. When he takes her hand from his face, her fingers feel cold, too. So he gently squeezes them. All the while, he's haunted by the cryptic private wish she whispered to Santa: *From a certain sweet guy, one special kiss … this Christmas.*

Still he's unsure as she sits close, her shawl loosely

draped, his scarf around her neck. Greg tucks her silky hair back, then lifts that shawl where it's dropped low on her shoulder. In all seriousness, he asks, "So you're warmer now?"

Lindsey nods. "With you next to me, I am."

Feeling her body close beside him—their legs touching, his hand brushing her bangs away from her gentle eyes—Greg nods, too. Nods, then turns to see Derek standing outside Snowflakes and Coffee Cakes, where he's talking to Vera and sipping a hot coffee.

Okay. So Greg can take this moment in one of two directions: call out to Derek and resume the horse-and-carriage ride, or heck, go in for that kiss. Cradle Lindsey's face, lean close and grant her wish—if only it were meant for him. Deepen their kiss, run his fingers through her soft hair, feel her hands touch his whiskered face, whisper close.

Instead? Greg hooks his fingers in his mouth and gives a sharp whistle.

As soon as he does, Derek quickly hugs Vera, then trots over to the carriage and unhitches the horse. "Where to, folks?" he asks while settling in the driver's seat and picking up the reins.

"Snowflake Lake," Greg tells him, leaning forward and clapping Derek's shoulder. "We'll get Lindsey home now."

When Derek shakes the reins, any romantic possibilities evaporate into the night's cold air.

Unable to look Lindsey in the eye then, Greg instead

turns his gaze on the passing sights. The horse's sleigh bells jingle-jangle as its hooves clip-clop through town. Their prearranged carriage ride takes them back down Main Street, across the wood-planked floor of the covered bridge, along Old Willow Road to the entrance of Snowflake Lake.

Ending the night … with all hearts intact.

twenty-one

LINDSEY GOT HER ANSWER.

According to her friend Penny, one little kiss would answer her pressing question: Is the feeling between Lindsey and Greg annoyance? Or is it a spark? One kiss is all it takes.

That's just fine, if you could *get* that kiss.

Even after sitting beside Greg when he played Santa Claus at the Merry Market, and then whispering her wish for one Christmas kiss from someone special, he didn't respond.

Even with every door open to a kiss on their arranged date—candlelit dinner beside a roaring fireplace, drinks, ambiance, romantic carriage ride—nothing.

Yes, Lindsey got her answer, all right.

It's painfully obvious that Dr. Greg Davis just isn't interested in her.

Busy packing up her tiny house on Friday evening, she scoops up her old-world Santa and sets it aside, out of the way of a few open cartons. "Oh, what was I thinking anyway?" she half says to the wise Santa statue. "It's time to hit the road. I'll get these last customer orders mailed tomorrow and be on my merry way." Giving a big sigh, she eyes the boxed merchandise stacked on her fold-down table—and overflowing onto one of the benches. "Addison was just a brief stop for a holiday stay. Nothing more."

With that, her tiny-house routine resumes. Prior to every journey, shelves need to be cleared. Loose items need to be secured for the road trip. This is strapped down; that is tied back. But with each strapping and tying today, Lindsey also trips on new inventory; or bumps into an added rack of boho clothes; or backs into her kitchenette counter and knocks off an extra bag of crocheted scarves that have been selling like, well, like hot cocoas!

Finally, she gets things under control—secured, locked down, tucked away and ready for highway travel. Her Merry Market stint is done and Christmas is just days away. With a glance at another messy pile of online orders stacked near the door, she thinks it'll be hard to leave this special town. But after mailing all those orders at the post office tomorrow and saying her goodbyes to a few familiar faces, there's nothing else keeping her here.

All that's left to do is apply the sticky address labels to her customers' shipping boxes. When she heads to the stack and begins shifting those boxes to her table, though, something that slipped behind them catches her eye.

Carefully, she lifts it up—lifts Greg's burgundy scarf.

With that one scarf in her hand, memories flood back from her time in the horse-drawn carriage a few nights ago. Their happy horse pranced them through the decorated town; passersby waved at them; carolers sang on street corners. Lindsey had sat close beside Greg in the carriage when he gently looped his scarf around her neck, then fussed with it, touching her hair, the skin of her face.

The thing is, whenever Lindsey's about to hitch up her tiny house and head for a new town, she doesn't like leaving behind any unfinished business. So after checking her watch, she decides now's as good a time as any to return the scarf to Greg. It'll give her the chance to say goodbye, too. She'll also apologize once more for backing her tiny house into his car, and for any annoying trouble it caused him these past few weeks.

Quickly, she puts on her suede coat and brimmed beanie, drops the folded scarf into a gift bag and settles into her unhitched SUV. It doesn't take long to drive across town to Greg's condo, where she parks at the curb and first looks up at the illuminated woodland Christmas tree in his living room window.

"It's nothing but a memory now," she says at the thought of decorating that tree. So she grabs the scarf bag, hurries up the back stairs to his door and stops there on the porch—bag in hand—about to knock.

⸙

Sitting on a chair in his bedroom, Greg laces up his trail boots. At least the holiday party at his brother's house will be casual, unlike the grand affair at the boathouse a few weeks ago. Boots, black jeans, gray V-neck cardigan over a button-down shirt cuffed at the sleeves—and he's good to go. This is more like it, he thinks while strapping on a heavy silver watch. Keeping things easy. Tonight's Christmas get-together at Wes and Jane's farmhouse should be pretty laid-back. Good food, a few laughs, great company.

Stopping in front of his mirror before heading out, Greg drags a hand through his somewhat overgrown hair, thinking he'll get a cut after Christmas. He draws his hand over his whiskered cheek, too, wondering how many days it's been since he last shaved.

"Eh," he says, waving off his reflection, shutting the bedroom light and hurrying through his condo. He swings into the kitchen, flips through a stack of envelopes and Christmas cards that came in the mail, then drops it all on the breakfast bar. Wes is expecting him early to give a hand with some of the food prep. So Greg lifts his leather bomber off a stool back, puts it on and grabs his car keys from the counter.

"Scarf, scarf," he whispers, looking around the kitchen for his burgundy scarf. The wind's been rattling the windows this evening, so it'd be nice to have that scarf around his neck. With no time to spare, he trots to the living room, switches on a table lamp and switches off the Christmas tree lights. His eyes scan the sofa, his cherry desk, an end table.

"Where the heck did I put that scarf?" he asks under his breath. But a glance at his watch tells him there's no time to look—not if he doesn't want to be late for his brother. So he zips up his black leather jacket, rushes to the door, whips it open—and crashes straight into Lindsey Haynes.

"Whoa! Whoa!" Greg says as he extricates himself from this woman with whom he shares a lengthy history of collisions. In a tangle of arms and hands and legs, he backs up and straightens his jacket … anything to get his bearings.

With a hand to her heart, Lindsey stands there wearing her coat and beanie, and holding a bag. "Greg!" she exclaims, pulling back and catching her balance after he nearly bowled her over.

Greg reaches out and steadies her. "I'm so sorry. I didn't know you were there."

"I was about to knock." Lindsey lifts the bag she holds. "Your scarf. I was returning it before I—"

"Right, you had it … from the other night. *That's* where it went! I was actually looking for it a minute—"

"It's just that, well, it's yours and I thought you should have—"

"Of course. Thank you for bringing …" He takes a breath, then a much longer one. "Lindsey." Her small smile is barely noticeable. Anyone else might miss it completely.

But *he* doesn't. And it makes him step back, tip his head and just listen to her soft voice.

"I came to say goodbye, too, Greg. And I … I wanted to thank you."

"Thank me?"

"Yes. To thank you for, well …" She looks away and then straight at him again. "For being a gentleman on our date. The auction date. You know."

Another slight smile that no one but Greg would notice. One that would break no one's heart but his.

"Because I'll be leaving soon," she whispers now, as though to say the words aloud might choke her up. "In a couple of days."

Okay. Greg stands there in his doorway looking at Lindsey Haynes standing on his porch step—flustered either from the cold, or from leaving town, or from their collision just now. A collision they still seem to be recovering from with their hesitations, glimpses, reluctant gestures.

The thing is—which Greg is very much aware of—the old Greg Davis would've invited Lindsey inside right about now. Would've helped her off with her coat, maybe had one last holiday toast with her. But heck, that was the old Greg Davis.

The new Greg Davis won't do that.

No, and here's why. For the first time in his life, the new Greg Davis is going to be late for a party.

That's right. Whatever happens now, happens. There is no plan. No strategy.

There is just an imminent kiss. One with no strings or hope attached. If it's just a kiss and nothing more, well, he's going to enjoy it and not let it bring down his holiday.

Without wasting another blessed second, the new Greg Davis simply goes for it, come what may. He and Lindsey have been fighting *this* collision for weeks now.

Greg hesitates for only a moment before taking a step closer to Lindsey. He says nothing, and neither does she. Instead, he reaches his hand out and lifts off her beanie, lightly brushing her mussed hair, too. "Lindsey," he says again, his voice low.

"I should go," she whispers, touching the sleeve of his leather bomber. "You were on your way out."

On his back porch, he steps closer, leans down and barely kisses first Lindsey's flushed cheek before pulling back, lifting a hand to her neck and kissing her again— this time on her lips. The night is quiet as he pulls her close. Kissing her outside his door, there is only the sound of their breaths, of the rustle of their coats, of the creak of a floorboard.

But then there's something else.

Lindsey pulls away and looks at him. The way her head is tipped, watching him, he can see her uncertainty. And, if he's not mistaken, her eyes well with tears.

So he leans down and touches her cheek just as she cautiously rises on her booted toes and raises her hand to his face, too. When he kisses her *this* time, there's no pulling back. This kiss is long, and deep.

It actually doesn't stop, either; instead, it moves. Because he can't keep himself from cradling her face and kissing her eyes, her cheek, her neck. When Lindsey's hands reach up and turn his face back to hers, when she kisses him as though her every breath depends on it, Greg does it.

Not stopping the kiss, he finagles the porch door open behind him and steps backward, getting inside his condo and pulling Lindsey in with him. Once they're inside where it's warm, and the lights dim, he nudges the door closed—kissing her still.

"Greg," he hears her murmur, their bodies close as he loosely pins her against the wall.

Which is when he lowers his hand to take the scarf bag she holds. He drops it behind him, then gently moves her heavy suede coat off her shoulders so that the coat falls to the floor, too.

The beauty of it all is that, no, the kiss never stops.

Not as he says her name right into her lips, not as her hands reach up around his shoulders, not as they slowly, with each lengthening second of that one kiss, sink together to the floor, on top of her coat, their embrace not once letting go—the kiss being all there is between them.

twenty-two

AN HOUR LATER, AFTER WALKING up the driveway filled two-deep with cars, Greg stands on the front porch of Wes and Jane's country farmhouse. Candlelit lanterns are on each step; twinkly lights wrap around the porch railing; a vintage barn star shines beneath tiny lights on the wooden front door. In the living room window, a grand Christmas tree glows.

But all Greg thinks, standing there in the dark and neatening his hair, tugging his leather bomber straight, is this: He and Lindsey just shared the kiss to end all kisses. And with her packed and getting ready to leave Addison, one thing's for certain: He'll never have another kiss like that one in all his livelong days.

Finally, he raises his hand, and as soon as he knocks on the door, Wes is opening it.

"Scrubs!" his brother says. "You were supposed to be here a half hour ago. And you're *never* late." Wes steps aside and looks past Greg's shoulder. "So what happened?"

"Eh. I got tied up." Greg drops his car keys into his pocket. "Couldn't get out the door."

He follows Wes inside to the foyer, where a potted red poinsettia sits on a white bench. Beyond, garland wraps around an oak banister leading up the staircase. Right away, there's the sound, too, of guests laughing and talking, their glasses clinking, music playing.

"Greg! I barely recognized you," Jane says, rushing to him and touching his cheek with a wink. "With all that scruff. Here, let me take your jacket."

When he turns and slips off his leather bomber, the festivities begin. His brother's farmhouse is a whirlwind that draws Greg right in. In the living room, a fire pops and crackles in the stone fireplace beside that grand, sparkling Christmas tree. For a few hours, Greg is as enmeshed as he can be with the guests there, with the friends, the food and drink, the laughs and caroling.

❧

Until at last, at the end of the night, Greg lands back at his condominium, alone.

Alone and looking at the scene of the crime. *Every* encounter with Lindsey these past few weeks somehow felt that way—each one took him by such surprise. You could put an orange cone at every single place they inadvertently collided.

Especially at the site of their final collision.

Problem is, that kiss was the most unexpected, and

emotional, collision of them all.

So, was that the Santa wish-kiss she'd wanted? Certainly seemed it. Or did they simply get caught up in a passionate moment of saying their last goodbye?

Greg hangs his jacket and scarf over a stool back at his kitchen island, then goes into the living room. There, he turns on the lights on his woodland Christmas tree. Standing beside the fragrant tree, he looks out his window to Main Street below. The Holly Trolley jingles by. Candles shine in neighboring homes' windows. A white picket fence is draped with garland and red bows.

Greg looks at it all, then turns back to his own Christmas tree and lightly touches a few branches. The balsam fir needles are as soft and gentle as, well, as Lindsey Haynes herself.

* * *

The way her emotions swirled and spun after that kiss, Lindsey's heart was fluttering like a snow flurry. Yes, like the very first flurries that fell just a few short weeks ago. So on her way home from Greg's condo, she stopped at Whole Latte Life. Something about the coffee shop's twinkling lights and cozy windows with their faux cottony snow tucked into the corners drew her in. She stepped inside, inhaled the pastry and coffee aromas, breathed a little deeper, then turned to the take-out counter to order a peppermint tea. She still felt too flustered to linger in a public place. So her plan was to bring the tea-to-go back to her tiny house, where she could sip it in solitude, with only her thoughts of Greg and their parting kiss.

But walking outside with the tea cupped in her mittened hands, one *jing-a-ling-ling* of a trolley bell changes everything.

"Lindsey?" Gus calls out from the Holley Trolley stopped curbside. The trolley's door is open as he leans over. "Is that you?"

"Oh. Hi, Uncle Gus."

"You're leaving town in a few days and haven't even had a trolley ride yet. Come aboard and I'll give you the grand holiday tour. Addison is so festive at night, with all the Christmas lights."

Though Lindsey only wants to go home to try to make sense of the kiss she just shared with Greg, she knows better than to argue with her uncle. So she climbs on and sits in a trolley seat behind Gus.

"What are you doing out at this hour?" he asks when he closes the trolley door and pulls back onto the road.

Lindsey sips her tea, piecing together her answer at the same time. "Before I leave here, there was something I had to return to Greg. Greg Davis?"

Gus nods as he glances at her in his rearview mirror, before turning his attention back to his driving.

"So I stopped by his place, and, well," she says, sipping her tea first, then dropping her voice. "I surely received something I *never* saw coming."

"Is that right?" With a raised eyebrow, Gus gives her a hopeful smile just as he pulls over to pick up more riders. Then, giving the trolley's bells a jingle, he calls out, "Off we go!"

As the trolley chugs along the streets, Lindsey thinks her favorite part of Gus' holiday tour is the road leading into Addison Cove. There's something so enchanting about the imposing houses, some of them historic ship captains' homes, others old bungalows and brick-front Tudors. Golden light spills from the windows; large, simple wreaths hang on wood-planked front doors; garland wraps up front-door pillars; candles flicker in paned windows. Even better, a sudden snow flurry drops spinning, glistening snowflakes from the cold, dark sky.

Seeing it all, and imagining that the homes look much the same now as they would have three hundred years ago, Lindsey thinks some things never change—whether it's the eighteenth century or the twenty-first. From day to day, century to century, you can count on the wonder of certain things, always. Holiday warmth. The comfort of home, sweet home. Falling snowflakes.

A kiss.

"Me and my Betty loved looking at the lights of Christmas together," Gus quietly tells her while driving that picturesque street to the cove. "It's really magical when you can share that with a special someone," he says, giving her a questioning glance in his mirror.

Lindsey only nods, then looks out her side window with a sigh. Just then, Gus turns the trolley around in the cove parking lot and makes the return trip back to Whole Latte Life. All the while, as the trolley rolls through this quaint New England town, dancing snowflakes and the twinkling Christmas lights of beautiful old homes whisk before Lindsey's very eyes.

The thing is? No *other* town she's ever landed in has ever made her feel right at home. No other residents have welcomed her so.

It's with that thought that she gets off the parked trolley, says goodnight to Gus and returns to her tiny house at Snowflake Lake … all alone.

twenty-three

As FAR AS GREG CAN see down the line of customers snaking back and forth across the post office lobby, everyone is holding at least one package. Wrapped in brown paper, or taped, or twined around and around, each box is destined to land beneath some Christmas tree in some living room, anywhere throughout the country. Fingers crossed that they arrive on time, no doubt, because it's already Saturday—with Christmas only three days away.

"Priority Mail must see a big upswing this time of year," Greg tells his father beside him. The two of them wait at the end of the line. Both men hold multiple wrapped boxes, some of Greg's nearly toppling.

"Glad I put in for this personal day months ago," Pete mentions. "Otherwise I'd be driving a mail truck *filled* with these packages and never get my last-minute Near and Deer orders shipped out."

When the next customer is called to the counter, the

extensive, ridiculously lengthy line inches forward ... starting with the first person and resulting in a forward motion moving like a wave through the customers behind.

Greg shifts his packages, gauges the wait and takes a long breath.

"What a shindig at Wesley's last night," Pete says. "And those red velvet cupcakes? Jane put out quite a spread of good eats."

"She sure did. I added a mile to my run this morning, just to burn off the calories." Another shuffling-forward as folks in coats and hats around them chat up the holiday—who's going where; who's having guests; what time should a turkey go in the oven; last-minute gift ideas. That idle holiday talk fills the room with a low hum.

When the post office door opens behind them, a gust of biting cold air blows in as someone maneuvers into the standing-room-only lobby. But whoever it is obviously can't see beyond the towering mountain of boxes in their arms and so bumps straight into Greg.

"Oh!" the woman says while scrambling to pick up a dropped package.

A minor commotion ensues as Greg bends to pick it up at the same time—and they bump again, jostling their wrapped-and-labeled packages.

"I'm *so* sorry," the woman tells him, looking up as their shoulders brush.

Wait.

The woman with long blonde hair, her bangs reaching

from beneath a slouchy brimmed-beanie to the top of her eyes.

The woman wearing a shearling-trimmed suede coat.

"We meet again, Miss Haynes," Greg says as he hands her the small box she dropped. "Or should I say … collide again?"

"So we do." Lindsey takes the package from him and steadies it on top of her armful of boxes. "Thank you. And sorry about that again."

"No problem." Greg watches her and shifts his own armful of boxes. "What are you up to this morning?"

Lindsey looks past him at the suddenly hushed roomful of customers. Greg glances that way too, just as a few people look back over their shoulders at them.

"Mailing the last of some holiday orders," Lindsey quietly explains. "My online customers love the clothes I featured in Addison photo shoots. Vagabond Vintage hasn't been busier."

"Next!" a postal clerk calls out, and the wave of inching-forward happens again.

"Same here," Greg tells Lindsey. "I'm helping my father mail off his Near and Deer packages before putting in a few hours at the hospital."

"Good to see you, Lindsey," Pete says then, somehow finagling a hand to briefly shake her own hand, which is wrapped around boxes, too. "Son!" Pete quickly looks over at Greg. "Hoist up your parcels. One's slipping."

As he hoists and shifts, Greg suddenly feels awfully warm. Warm enough to somehow unzip his leather bomber and loosen his scarf, barely, before catching a box from toppling. All the while, one thing becomes even more obvious. The amount of holiday chitchat has oddly dwindled in the post office lobby. Folks are unusually quiet now.

"Lindsey," Greg says, keeping his voice low while hitching his head. "Why don't you go ahead of us?"

When he backs up, Lindsey squeezes past him with her arms full. "Thanks," she whispers.

"*Next*, please! Over here," another postal clerk calls out while waving to the customers in line.

And so the post-office-lobby-shuffle begins again as everyone takes a few steps forward in succession.

"Have any plans for Christmas, Lindsey?" Pete asks, leaning around his boxes. "Heading anywhere special?"

"I'm actually leaving Christmas Eve morning. On Monday. I'll be at my parents' house for the holidays. And *oh*," she says, tapping Pete's arm, "I can't *wait* to give them the whittled deer! They'll just love them. Then after Christmas, I'm on the road again, heading south this time."

Greg's not sure what does it, but even Pete quiets after she answers. Maybe it's that his father will be sad to see Lindsey go. Or, Greg suspects, maybe it's the now-awkward silence filling the lobby that quiets Pete. Too many heads are tipped noticeably so, eavesdropping on their talk. When Greg looks at Lindsey, she gives him a slight smile and seems a little flushed as she moves to the head of the line.

"Next, miss!" the clerk calls to her.

Lindsey carries her packages to the counter in a pin-drop silence that Greg's never before heard in the post office. Someone's always got *something* to say to somebody else. When he walks past Lindsey a minute later to get to the next available clerk, Greg tells her, "It was good seeing you last night, Lindsey."

She looks long at him, obviously knowing full well that he's referring to their encounter, right in his condo doorway. But she can only nod here—with a full audience enraptured by their every move.

"You take care now," Greg says. "Safe travels."

"Happy holidays," Lindsey answers back, hesitating before turning to her transaction at the counter.

Every few seconds, though, Greg glances over at her standing at the clerk's window beside his. When she leaves minutes later, she glances his way, too, meeting his eye. And he has to admit, he's surprised—and glad—when she backtracks and hurries to him, standing close beside him at the counter.

"Oh, and Greg?" Lindsey reaches out and gives his hand a quick squeeze as his clerk is stamping and organizing all the Near and Deer packages.

"What is it?" Greg asks, concerned now.

She leans a little closer. "Thanks for making my Christmas wish come true last night," she nearly whispers, then walks away with only a glance back.

"Anything else?" his clerk asks.

Greg looks at the clerk, then back to Lindsey. Christmas

wish? The kiss? So it *was* meant for him, after all.

"Stamps today, sir?"

Greg turns to the clerk again. "No, not today."

Funny thing is, Greg notices how the chattering in the room picks up—slightly, but growing in volume—as soon as Lindsey starts to leave. The chatter comes in whispers first, then hushed talk. And he doesn't miss a beat of it.

> *Is she the one who hit him?*
> *Didn't they go on that auctioned date?*
> *Are they seeing each other?*
> *Her tiny house collided with his car!*
> *She's leaving town? Too bad!*

Greg waits there at the counter as Pete pays the clerk and they finish up mailing the customer packages. But now? Now the walls feel like they're closing in on Greg— a little more so with each cupped and leaning whisper. He's warm in the stuffy lobby, and so hurries outside to the cold air before his father is even done returning his wallet to his pocket and checking the receipt. Greg doesn't wait, and instead walks alone across the parking lot to his black Mustang Fastback.

As soon as Pete eventually opens the passenger door, Greg starts the engine.

And as soon as Pete sits in the low-slung seat, Greg's peeling out—barely giving his father time to close the door. In seconds, they're a mere block away from the traffic roundabout.

"Now *focus*, son," Pete says. "You can't be hesitant."

"Dad." Greg yields to oncoming traffic and waits for an opening to merge in. "Don't be hesitant?" he asks with a sidelong glare at his father. "I *know* how to drive, okay?"

Pete is quiet for a second, before saying, "Wasn't talking about driving."

"What?" A horn beeps, and Greg checks his rearview mirror, still not pulling into the roundabout. "Okay. Okay, Dad. I *get* it," he says, glancing at his father again. "It's Lindsey, isn't it?"

His father simply turns up his hands.

That's all it takes. His father silently admitting the truth of things.

The truth of Lindsey Haynes.

Well now. Here's a dilemma and it might change everything.

Change everything for Greg, at least. The old Greg Davis … oh, he thought he knew what love was—with all its courting and planning and romantic dates.

But the old Greg Davis, come to find out, was wrong.

Because the new Greg Davis? The new Greg Davis feels a flurry in his heart that he's *never* felt before. That feeling is light. And free. It spins and dances, lifting his spirit in a way that is so unfamiliar to him.

An opening comes in the roundabout traffic and Greg carefully maneuvers in his Mustang. As he does, he glances at his father in the passenger seat once, then again. "I get it that you're talking about Lindsey … and that scene back there in the post office. But there's something you *don't* know, Dad." Greg waits a long moment before saying what he *never* saw coming this holiday season. "I think I'm falling in love with her."

"That's wonderful!" Pete reaches over and pats Greg's shoulder. "I only want to see my sons happy!"

"But here's the thing, Dad," Greg says as he circles the roundabout. "I'm *not* happy."

"What? Why not?"

Greg exits the roundabout. The Mustang's engine rumbles as he picks up speed and heads to his father's old Victorian house. "Lindsey's a free spirit, traveling from place to place in her tiny house," Greg explains. "She's always been up-front about that. The road calls to her, and she maps out all these far-flung destinations to explore," he says, motioning to the street ahead. "You heard her."

Problem is, Greg did, too. Christmas wishes or not, love or not—it's not enough to keep her here. "In two days, she'll be on the highway again," Greg reminds Pete … and himself. "So who am I to lasso her? To rope her in here, in our one little town of Addison?"

❦

Her shingled tiny house is quiet today. Vagabond Vintage is closed and shuttered until after the holidays. The online orders are mailed. Her mannequin is secured; the old-world Santa stands alone near the door. There's not even a wintry wind rattling the windows. Just a soft quiet fills the space.

Lindsey doesn't play any records on her turntable while packing to leave. Something about music doesn't suit her oddly heavy heart. As she straps back merchandise; and trips on a pair of Doc Marten boots she'd added to her vintage inventory; and topples a towering stack of used books; and bumps into an empty storage tote, something feels … off.

One thing that always cheers her up is her corkboard map. So she hurries to where it hangs near her fold-down table and scoops some pushpins from her pin mug. Eyeing the pin-dotted map, she presses in a few green pushpins along her upcoming southern route. Already the vendor-confirmation emails are filling her inbox.

"New Jersey," she whispers with the first pin as she tries to think ahead to her next shop-stops. "Delaware. North Carolina."

A sudden knock on her tiny house door stops her though. It's Penny, rushing in. "I'm glad I caught you before you left," she says, somewhat out of breath. "I have a gift for you, Linz."

"Aw, you didn't have to."

"But I wanted to. It's just a little something for Christmas. Because I'm really glad to have met you," Penny says while handing Lindsey the festively wrapped gift, "and I'm sad to see you leave. Open it!"

Lindsey's not sure why, but that heavy heart of hers returns in full force, especially when she unwraps a lovely silver-mesh wristwatch. It blurs beneath the tears she blinks back.

"It's to remember all your *time* here in Addison," Penny explains as she sits at the fold-down table and takes off her pom-pom hat. "We'll all miss you."

Her time here in Addison? There's something so special about it. Oh how her days in Addison passed—surprising and magical and wonderful—each day like a unique, falling snowflake. Lindsey puts on the watch and runs a finger across its face. "Of all the places I've parked my tiny house this past year, I'm not sure why, Penny, but Addison is the very hardest place to leave behind."

After a quiet moment, Penny asks, "Maybe you don't have to?"

There's no one else here Lindsey can talk to. No one like her lakeside friend, Penny. So Lindsey sits across from her at the table. Sinks slowly onto the bench seat. "I have to tell you something, too," she admits.

"What?"

"You won't believe it." A pause, then, "I have my answer. There *was* a spark."

"Wait. Wait! Back it up, girlfriend. Because if there was a *spark*," Penny says while leaning across the table, "then there was … a kiss?"

Lindsey nods, but with no smile. "To end all kisses."

"Oh my gosh!" As she says it, Penny nearly leaps out of her seat, but then squints at Lindsey and sits back down. "So … what's the problem?"

"That kiss leaves me with more questions than answers. I mean, well, I only stopped at Greg's to drop off his scarf. And it just … happened. The kiss."

227

Having told no one about her kiss with Greg, it all comes vividly back to her as she shares the details. Lindsey can picture that kiss as though on replay: Greg leaning in close, clasping her neck, her fingers touching his whiskered face, his mouth on hers as they somehow got off the porch and inside to his kitchen, where it happened—that gradual, delicious sinking to the floor as Greg moved closer, pressed back her hair, bent low over her, the kiss slowly deepening.

"Then," Lindsey whispers, "just as quickly, it ended."

"Ended?"

"Ended. Greg was on his way out when I'd gotten there. He had his coat on, his keys in his hand. So he *really* had to leave. But … the spark? *That* didn't go out."

"Well." Penny looks around the tiny house before her gaze locks onto Lindsey again. "You can't drive away leaving things like this between you two!"

"But I'm not a hundred percent sure. *Was* it a spark? Or was it just an impulsive, emotional farewell kiss?"

"You have to talk to him."

"I did, at the post office earlier. He wished me well, Penny, on my journey. And that's it. No hint of anything else."

"Nothing? He didn't say to keep in touch, or drop him a line even?"

"No." Lindsey swipes at an escaped tear. "Geez Louise. I don't know why I'm so upset. I mean … it's not like we're in *love* or something." Lindsey gives her friend a small smile across the table. "And anyway, I'm leaving." She motions to the tied-back shelves and packed totes

228

and cartons tucked into storage spaces. "Vagabond Vintage is booked after the holidays, all winter long. I have firm commitments at markets and vendor fairs down south. So I need to hit the road."

"But how? How can you even travel? Because I've told you already, Linz. You're bursting at the seams here. This tiny house has nowhere *near* enough room for all your beautiful treasures! And I saw you at the Merry Market. There were lines out your door! And not enough dressing rooms. Your business is really growing, and you *can't* ignore that. So hear me out. I have an idea …"

"What are you getting at, Penny?"

"It's hard to explain." Penny abruptly stands, grabs a silk scarf from a basket and takes Lindsey's hand. "Come with me."

"Where?" Lindsey asks while quickly slipping into her coat and brimmed beanie.

Penny yanks her outside into the late-afternoon chilly air, pulls her across the pathway toward Cardinal Cabin, but veers off to her car. She nudges Lindsey into the passenger seat. "Lindsey Haynes?" she asks. "*You* are my holiday hostage. Here," she instructs as she hands Lindsey the silk scarf she took from the tiny house. "Cover your eyes. And get ready for a surprise!"

～○

With that silk scarf over her eyes, Lindsey feels every bump in the frost-heaved road leaving Snowflake Lake.

From driving her tiny house to the Merry Market every day, she actually knows the entire terrain of the town now. Knows the gentle curve of Old Willow Road. The stop-and-go hesitations of the roundabout.

Now she hears the *plunk-plunk-plunk* of the car's tires on the covered bridge, and moments later, hears the rising song of carolers. So she can figure they are somewhere on Main Street, where those carolers are serenading passing shoppers.

Finally, Penny pulls over and parks her car curbside. "Don't say *anything* until I explain," she insists when she leans over and lifts the silk scarf off Lindsey's eyes. "Wait. Deep breath first. Now visualize Vagabond Vintage on historic Main Street."

"What?" Lindsey looks from Penny, then out through the windshield, where every storefront is chock-full of Christmas décor, and gifts, and bakery items, and children's toys.

Every store except the vacant one Penny points to now.

"See that big display window?" Penny asks. "It's perfect for your mannequins all dressed in those amazing vintage clothing pieces you find. And, even better," she says, nodding her head to the bare storefront, "it's *still* a tiny place, so you'll be comfortable there."

Lindsey looks out her passenger window at the empty shop. It's in a white-painted brick building with forest-green awnings. The building's downstairs is actually divided into two shops. On the left side there's a travel agency. Twinkly lights frame its window where travel posters depict the perfect snowy lodges and mountain cabins to visit for the holidays.

On the building's right side, there is a vacant space. Its bay window is multipaned, and also empty. Beyond it, the room inside is dark.

Lindsey whips around and looks at Penny then.

As though she knows just what Lindsey might say, Penny holds up a mittened hand. "Hear me out! It's a small place, I know. But it's still bigger than your tiny house. It used to be a candy shop, but that went out of business and the store's been vacant for *months* now."

"What's that got to do with me?" Lindsey asks.

Penny nods to the FOR RENT sign in the corner of the window, then gets out of the car and goes around to Lindsey's side right as she gets out, too.

"No," Lindsey says while tipping up the brim of her slouchy beanie and squinting over at the store. "Staying put in one place is *not* how I operate. I'm more of a daydreamer, Penny. Footloose. That's why my shop's on *wheels.*"

"But it doesn't have to be. Not anymore. May I remind you how much Vagabond Vintage has *really* outgrown your tiny house? Every time you turn around, you're bumping this, or jostling that. And … and … you can still *live* in your tiny house, and use it for flea-market and tag-sale trips, scouring for new shop items. Not to mention, the townsfolk here just *love* your store. How many times have you restocked because they practically clean out your inventory? So this spot could be perfect." Penny pulls Lindsey to the paned window. "Best of all? I work next door at Suitcase Escapes!"

"No, I can't," Lindsey persists. "I'm leaving in two days. My map's all pinned with reserved stops."

"Just wait here." Penny rushes toward the side of the building. "The landlady lives upstairs. We can take a *look*, at least," she calls out before rounding the corner of the building and heading toward a back entrance.

Helplessly, Lindsey watches her go. On the cobblestone sidewalk, shoppers brush past her in their last-minute rush. She watches them, then steals a glance through the vacant store's paned window. It's dark inside and hard to see any details. Shaking her head, she steps away and looks across the street to where the town Christmas tree soars on The Green. It's getting late, and she really needs to finish packing up her things at home. But as she thinks it, she's cupping her hands to the shop's glass door and trying to see inside again.

Which is exactly how Penny finds her when she returns with the landlady, who's wearing a mid-length cape over her booted jeans—and holds a key ring in her hand.

"Happy to show you around," the woman says while unlocking the shop's door.

It's cold inside the empty store, and Lindsey huddles into her coat as she crosses the creaky wooden floor. Penny and the landlady chat behind her. From the sounds of it, Penny's telling her all about Vagabond Vintage. Their voices are hushed as Lindsey squints into the shop's shadows.

It's currently run out of a tiny house.
Really! I think I saw it at the Merry Market?
That's the one. It's on wheels, so Lindsey's kept her business mobile.

Their footsteps and voices echo against the bare walls—where Lindsey brushes her fingers across old wood shelves perfect for displaying handbags. A stark ceiling light casts a glow on timeworn counters. Those have glass tops and are framed with a dark wood that would only need a polishing to bring back their sheen. They're the type of old-style counters she can just imagine customers slightly bending at, pointing out some turquoise bracelet behind the glass, or tortoise-framed sunglasses, or fine silk scarf.

Oh, she's no fool, either. Lindsey knows exactly what it all is, too. Knows what *everything* is in this vacant store that gets her visualizing. And yes, daydreaming.

Because it's everything she's *dreamt* about but could never fit inside her tiny house.

But it doesn't matter. For the next few months, her life's already mapped out—pushpin by pushpin—leading her down the coast, one definite stop at a time.

"A boutique *would* fit in well here," the landlady is saying. "Folks could stop in and get the perfect outfit for a trip they just booked next door at Suitcase Escapes."

"I'm not sure it can work," Lindsey tells her.

As she does, though, Lindsey can't keep her gaze off the shop details: the bay window where she'd arrange mannequins in fun seasonal displays; the drab ceiling light that she'd replace with a sparkling crystal chandelier; the alcove perfect for *legitimate* dressing rooms.

"I have commitments to other towns," Lindsey vaguely says instead, "where there are spaces reserved just for my tiny pop-up shop, Vagabond Vintage." She gazes about and pictures actual garment racks displaying her vintage clothing here. A vast improvement to her inventory now crammed into plastic crates. "You know, *vagabond*, because I wander from place to place … and there's my map, with pushpins … different destinations …"

But—she doesn't let on—with the way her shop's been so weighed down recently? There's also a risk for tire blowouts while driving the interstates. New worries like that one she keeps to herself. Not to mention, life on the road can get awfully lonely, too.

When her words drift off, the landlady looks over with a kind smile. "You know? Things sometimes work in mysterious ways," she tells Lindsey. "I don't need an answer today, okay? You get some Christmas clarity first."

Christmas clarity?

As Penny drives her back through town to Snowflake Lake, the charming sights blur before Lindsey's eyes. Pretty white lights and candlelit colonial windows and garland-draped white picket fences pass by—twinkling and beautiful and *fleeting* … now that she'll soon be leaving them all behind.

So this drive through town is bittersweet.

In her carefree, footloose life that's been mapped out with pushpins and assorted delightful destinations to land in, the town of Addison today feels like one misty cloud of confusion, swirling Lindsey in a tearful flurry of uncertainty.

twenty-four

WHAT'S NICE ABOUT DOING LAST-MINUTE things is this: It means the busyness is done. Last-minute things are like putting a finishing touch on a painting, or pulling a wayward weed from a tended garden. The hard work is behind you. All that's left is fussing … tinkering.

By Sunday afternoon, Lindsey is doing just that—tinkering with her packed and secured tiny house. This morning she double-checked the house's trailer lights and brakes to ensure safe travels. After that, to prepare for highway driving, she tightens straps inside the rooms, tapes shut a carton of kitchen glassware and removes almost all artwork from the walls. The one piece left hanging until it's time to leave is the pushpin map.

As Lindsey tinkers—storing cartons beneath the loft stairs, transferring her own wardrobe to her SUV's cargo area, moving her snowman snow globe to the SUV'S cup holder—she does something else, too.

She thinks.

Thinks about Greg Davis. There's been no word from him since they bumped into each other yesterday in the post office. Nothing at all—not an offer of a holiday coffee, not another farewell—and she *can* be easily found.

So that's that.

Their unexpected kiss was simply an emotional goodbye after several random run-ins during the past few weeks. She knows it's all for the best as their lives are so different. Let's face it, he's an orthopedic surgeon well established here in Addison.

And Lindsey? She intends to hitch up her tiny house tomorrow morning and hit the road. First stop … spending the holidays with her parents. After that, Lindsey will cruise the highways and byways again, headed to her next pushpin location, further south.

As she gives her tiny house one last pre-highway safety check, a motion outside catches her eye. It's her uncle Gus filling the bird feeders for the cardinals. So she puts on her coat and beanie and goes outside, too, calling to him as she approaches.

"I want to say goodbye, Uncle Gus. I'll be leaving early tomorrow."

Gus sets down the sack of black-oil sunflower seeds. He also tips up his cap and looks her straight on. "Are you *sure* you want to leave? You can invite your parents here for Christmas, you know. Chickadee Shanty is vacant, with plenty of room for them. And *I'd* love to see my brother, too."

Lindsey, with her hands in her pockets, shakes her

head. "No." She tips up her face. "Feel those winter winds? They're winds of change, Uncle Gus, moving me on in my vagabond life. Tomorrow it's time for me to leave. All that's left to do is gas up my SUV."

When Gus opens his arms to her, she walks right into his embrace, feeling him pat her back. He tells her he'll miss having her around, and that there's nothing quite like having family nearby.

Always being on the go, one thing Lindsey's perfected is the quick exit. So after she hugs Gus back and leaves a kiss on his cheek, she hurries off to her little shingled house. Since her coat's already on, she just grabs her car keys from the table so she can hit the gas station now. That way, first thing tomorrow, she's free to go.

Headed to her door, though, she stops short. The old-world Santa she found curbside just a few weeks ago stands there, his burlap sack slung over his shoulder, his white beard hanging over his long burgundy robe, his wise face seeming to watch her.

And sadly, Lindsey knows what she has to do. It's her last piece of unfinished business. So she digs Santa's twined cardboard sign out of a drawer, scoops Santa up and brings him outside to her vehicle, too.

"There's no room for you here," she says as she stands him in the front passenger seat. "Everything I have is so crammed into my tiny house. And there's no attic in my tiny life either … no place to store Christmas decorations." When she loops the seatbelt across her wise old Santa to secure him in place, she remembers how

237

Greg did the same thing the day they first unintentionally collided.

No, there'll be none of that now.

Quick exit, Lindsey reminds herself. She has no use for nostalgic memories, for bittersweet thoughts that will only make it even harder to leave. There's something more pressing that needs to be done instead.

Driving down the rutted, frost-heaved, one-lane road out of Snowflake Lake, Lindsey turns onto Old Willow Road. A block later, she carefully pulls over beside an old oak tree, parks and gets out. This spot will do. There's plenty of traffic here; cars with many onlookers drive by all day. Lovely old homes line the street, too—homes with families that might welcome a special decoration. So she unbuckles Santa from the passenger seat and sets him firmly at the curb. Rushing back to her vehicle, she reaches in for his cardboard sign.

"Someone will pick you up," she says when she reads the original plea that came with her roadside find: *Santa Needs A New Home! FREE*. Looping the sign around the old-world Santa's shoulders, she admits, "*You're* destined to stay right here in Addison ... but I'm not."

After patting his head with a whispered *Goodbye*, she walks back to her SUV. Once inside, she looks regretfully at Santa in her rearview mirror. His burgundy velvet robe blows in the wind, and his long white beard wafts a bit, too. Feeling wistful, she pulls onto the road without another teary glance back.

Though her tears fade, Lindsey can't quell a certain

sadness. This may be the last time she drives down Addison's country streets of gingerbread houses and sweet little storefronts. So there's a sense of farewell to her drive today.

Once at the gas station, the last item on her pre-trip checklist awaits: Fill her SUV's tank. Tomorrow, she'll simply hitch up her tiny house and be on her way.

"Done," she says with reluctant finality after paying the attendant and hurrying back inside her vehicle.

But when she starts up the SUV, she idles right there at the pump for a few seconds before pulling over to the side of the gas station lot. Her vehicle faces the road, giving her a clear view of this quintessential New England town. Of the boutiques with silver-garland-draped store windows. Of the cobblestone sidewalks shoppers hurry along. Of the coach-light lampposts topped with red velvet bows.

In a moment, her eyes stop on the snowman snow globe she'd earlier set in her cup holder for the trip ahead. She wipes a persistent tear from her eye, then picks up the snow globe and gives it a shake. A delicate snow flurry falls around the snowman inside it. His burgundy scarf blows; his cute snowman face seems to watch her with anticipation.

"I just don't know," Lindsey whispers, then gives the snow globe another shake. "*Unsure where to go?*" she still whispers, reciting her father's verse. But when she says it this time, new tears also streak her cheek. "*Give a little shake … and your heart will always know.*"

She watches the snow flurry falling around the snowman in her globe. The swirling flakes look just like the flurries starting outside her windshield. Looking up at the sky now, those real snowflakes swirl and spin, tumbling down from gray clouds.

Suddenly, the sight of these white snowflakes falling all around? Snowflakes dusting rooftops and porch railings and shoppers' coats? Those flakes, well, they get Lindsey to smile. Because, looking out from behind her windshield, it's as though she's in her very own, real-*life* snow globe.

Why … it's all a bit of Christmas magic that touches her heart.

A bit of *snowflake* magic that has her put her SUV in gear, drive a few blocks past decorated boutiques and the charming coffee shop, hit the blinker and turn into the parking lot of one particular storefront.

A very familiar, very *empty* storefront that she gazes at from her driver's seat.

An empty storefront that she imagines filled—wall to wall, glass counter to glass counter—with vintage treasures of all kinds. Retro jeans stacked neatly on honest-to-goodness actual shelves. Patterned scarves hung on wall pegs. A bell that jingles each time a customer walks in.

A shop that she sees with a new clarity as the Christmas snowflakes continue to fall.

In the midst of all of them, Lindsey gets out of her SUV and first tips her laughing face up to the magical, snowy sky. Then, with more tears—these ones of happiness—she runs around to the landlady's back door, stops and raises her hand.

It worked, again. Her cherished snowman snow globe didn't let her down.

Give a little shake ... and your heart will always know, Lindsey thinks.

And it does.

After only a moment's hesitation, she nods. Nods, reaches around a festive balsam wreath and gives an excited *knock-knock-knock* on the wood-planked door.

twenty-five

WHAT DID IT GET HIM?

It's a thought stuck in Greg's head Monday morning. He'd sat out the holiday love season. Benched all attempts at romance. Canned any casual dates.

Yes, he'd convinced himself it was the only way to get through Christmas with his heart in one piece. Keeping himself out of the game would keep his heart intact. No lovelorn cracks would break that heart in two—if only he shielded it from the sidelines.

So why's he feeling so down? It's Christmas Eve morning after all, and he's sitting in his condo kitchen with a steaming mug of coffee. No guy stole the girl right from under his eyes this year, because this year he was darn sure not to *have* a girl.

"You happy now?" he asks himself before switching on the countertop TV. When he sits again, he checks his watch. No doubt, right about now Lindsey Haynes has her tiny house all hitched to her SUV and is leaving

Snowflake Lake. She's probably driving along that rutted, heaved, one-lane road—her shingled house tipping this way, jostling that way. Eventually, she'll make it to Old Willow Road, straight through town to the interstate highway … leaving Addison behind.

Footloose and fancy-free, that's the life she's chosen.

On the TV screen, meteorologist Leo Sterling wears his snowflake tie and is spewing some random snowflake lore. "Last night's halo around the moon … means lots of snow's coming—and soon!"

Even Leo can't get a smile out of Greg.

Because Greg's grand plan failed. There's no denying that his holiday heart, this Christmas Eve day, is heavy. Maybe it's time to tap into the old Greg Davis. Because, heck, the old Greg Davis would've found a way to justify Lindsey's departure. The old Greg Davis, as an Rx for his unexpectedly sad heart, might have written a little list of reasons she's leaving town.

So that's what the new Greg Davis will do, too. Grabbing a small notepad from a drawer, he sits at his kitchen island and thinks of what he could jot in bulleted and dashed and numbered lists. Everything is considered—from Lindsey being a traveling daydreamer on the hunt for all things vintage, to her very specific pushpin map designating each destination.

By the time Greg's about to put his pencil to paper, Leo Sterling is finishing his winter lore segment. "Though it's been weeks since the season's very first flurry, more snow is coming today—so get out your shovels in a hurry!"

And by the time Greg's finished his coffee, brushed a hand across his unshaven face and put on his leather bomber, not only is that sheet of paper still blank and tossed in the trash, so is that pencil he'd intended to use.

Because one thing's for certain: He's *not* the old Greg Davis, writing off another solo holiday season.

No. Greg hoists his jacket around his shoulders, loops on his scarf and zips that leather bomber.

The new Greg Davis, yes, he's going for it—just like he did with that kiss. As he swipes his keys off the counter, he doesn't have much of a plan like the old Greg Davis would have. And that's fine, all fine.

Instead, he only has a shred of hope as he gets in his Mustang Fastback and roars through Addison's streets toward Snowflake Lake.

The smallest scrap of hope that Lindsey hasn't hitched her tiny house and left town yet.

❦

All hopes are dashed, though, when Greg steers his '68 Mustang along Old Willow Road. Dashed and doused with a good dose of regret when he sees Lindsey's wise old-world Santa standing curbside with its *FREE* sign fluttering in the winter wind. Santa's burgundy robe flutters, too, as tiny snowflakes start to dust his shoulders.

Slamming on the brakes, Greg wrangles his skidding-and-fishtailing Mustang to a stop. With his car idled but crooked at the curb, he runs out, grabs up the Santa statue and leans to the side, squinting down the street for even a glimpse of a departing, shingled tiny house. Did Lindsey just *now* leave? Or have hours passed since she stopped and set her cherished Santa Claus roadside? Giving a sad shake of his head, he realizes there would be no storage space in her tiny house for a large decoration like this one. With that thought, Greg buckles Santa into the Mustang's passenger seat.

It's the least he can do.

Yes, Greg will give Santa a new home. He'll stand him in his condo's living room, near the fireplace. And every time he looks at the wise old Santa, it'll remind him of the girl who passed through his life like a mystical snow flurry—landing here suddenly one December day—before just as suddenly breezing away.

As he walks around his car and opens the driver's door, a familiar sound grows louder. It's the sputtering *putt-putt-putt* of Gus' approaching snowtorcycle.

"Greg!" Gus calls out. He parks behind the black Mustang and motions Greg over.

"It's starting to snow," Greg says as he closes his car door and walks to Gus. "Where you headed in this messy weather?"

"Picking up fresh pies from the farm stand. Placed a Christmas order, special for the grandkids. They'll be here tonight for Christmas Eve!" Gus leans over and eyes the Mustang parked haphazardly at the curb—right before the turnoff to Snowflake Lake. "More importantly, where are *you* headed? To see someone special?"

"Someone special who I apparently missed." After telling Gus how he rescued Lindsey's old-world Santa from the curb, Greg turns up his hands in defeat. "She's gone, and must've left Santa behind on her way out."

"Gone? I know Lindsey was *planning* to hitch up her house and hit the road. But," Gus pauses with—if Greg's not mistaken—a twinkle in his eye. "I'm pretty sure she's still here." He nods toward that frost-heaved, one-lane road leading to Snowflake Lake. Giving a rev of his snowtorcycle engine, he calls out, "If anyone's ever been granted a Christmas miracle, I think you have, Dr. Davis."

Greg stares at Gus, just for a second, though. Just until he gives Gus a quick thanks, runs to his car and guns his Mustang—fishtailing down that beautiful, heaved, one-lane road. When he gets to the end and turns off, there's Lindsey Haynes' shingled tiny house right where he'd never dreamt it would be—still parked between two tall pine trees, their boughs snow-dusted and sweeping low.

Well now. Now Greg feels every single beat of his heart. Is it about to be broken? Or will it be filled with holiday happiness? He won't know if he doesn't set it free to find out.

So he slowly drives over to the tiny house, parks and sits there for a moment. Snow falls softly around the hushed lake. The tiny flakes faintly cover his windshield, too. Not wasting any more time, Greg gets out, retrieves Santa from the passenger seat and carries him toward the little shingled house. At the edge of the lake, wild grasses bend beneath the crystal-white snowflakes. Beyond, on a trail in the woods, a rickety footbridge crosses over a babbling brook. All around the lake, little wood cabins are strung with garland; smoke curls from chimneys; the lakeside Christmas tree is aglow in twinkling lights. All of it, all around, is quiet. There is only the sound of his footsteps as Greg walks a stone path to that little shingled house nestled among the trees.

With the Santa statue tucked beneath his arm, he picks up his pace—well aware that the old Greg Davis would've cleared his throat and brushed back his hair along the way. Would've fidgeted with his gloves at the door. Would've actually *knocked* on that tiny house door.

But that was the old Greg Davis.

The new Greg Davis? He rushes up the few steps to the tiny house, opens the door and walks right in.

∽

Greg had no plan. No thought as to what he'd say. All he knew, the whole way here, was that he *had* to see Lindsey. Standing there now in his bomber, scarf and trail boots, he knows why, too: He wanted one more—just *one*—unintentional collision.

Still holding the old-world Santa, Greg doesn't move once he sees Lindsey standing in front of her corkboard wall map. She's wearing a fitted black sweater over flared jeans and, surprisingly, she's methodically pulling all the pushpins out of her beloved map. But she stops and quickly turns around when she hears him come in. "Greg. What are you doing here?"

"Lindsey," he says.

Lindsey drops a pin in the empty cocoa mug she holds, all while watching him.

"What are *you* doing?" Greg asks, stepping closer. "Your pins … your map."

As sudden tears streak Lindsey's cheeks, she reaches back to the map hung above her fold-down table and pulls out another pin. "Don't you see?" she asks over her shoulder.

"No." He takes another step closer in her tiny house crammed with taped boxes and overflowing bags.

Lindsey slightly turns, and from beneath her blonde bangs, she looks at him. Oh, and he knows just what she sees. It's certainly not the sight of the old Greg Davis. The thought of *that* has Greg quickly drag a hand through his overgrown, windblown hair, and brush snowflakes off his leather bomber. Okay, there's nothing he can do about the whiskers on his face. All the while, Lindsey gives him a once-over before pulling out more map pins and dropping them into her cup—each dropped pin making a soft clink.

Greg shifts the old-world Santa beneath his arm. "You can't do this, Lindsey. Those pins, they're marking your journey. Right?" He steps closer again, nearing the framed map. "Don't you follow the wind … and those places were next?" he asks, pointing to the southernmost pins.

Silently, Lindsey shakes her head. She continues pulling out every single red and green pushpin—except for one lone pin. "Listen," she says, then picks up a marker and starts drawing a line on her map.

"Lindsey, you're ruining your *map*. Why?"

When she glances at him this time, it's with a small smile. The tears are still there, but they're different now.

"Watch," she whispers.

From behind her shoulder, he does. Carefully. The tiny house is silent as she raises her arm. Her marker moves along the map from one pushpin-dot to another. The marker goes to each tiny dot where there'd previously been a pin. The line she draws zigs and meanders—from dot to dot, up and down, east and west—in one complicated route.

"In each place, I stopped," Lindsey explains, still connecting the dots in a line. "I set up my tiny shop. I met people, saw some of the country. And each time, I was always ready to move on. Until now." She lifts her marker off the map and looks back at him. "So I'm not."

"What?"

"Come to find out, I wasn't *randomly* roaming for the past year." She tucks her hair behind an ear, studies her map, then turns to him again. Her smile, though slight, is undeniable. "I was on this incredible journey, even if I didn't know it. A journey to find the right home for my tiny house ... my tiny life."

"A home?" Greg asks. "I don't get it."

When she looks at him this time, her tears are clearly happy. Greg can tell by that smile, too, and the way her eyes sparkle. "I was on a journey, it's true. A journey to an empty

249

little storefront perfect for Vagabond Vintage … right *here*," she whispers, just as she touches the one remaining pin on her map. "An empty boutique on Main Street. In a town I've simply fallen in love with. One with friends and family close by, too. So you see? My journey actually led my tiny house up and down the coast, in and out of states and counties, to a special lakeside spot between two pine trees … for a reason. It led my tiny house home."

Greg carefully sets down the old-world Santa, then walks to Lindsey and brushes a strand of hair off her face. "Are you saying …?"

It's been said that a picture's worth a thousand words. But to Greg, in this silent moment when Lindsey—pretty Lindsey who backed her tiny house into his car, and into his life—looks only at him and gently nods, that *nod* is worth a thousand words. And those words all come together in his thoughts, in wonder. How can it be that in this year when he all but gave up on finding someone, when he didn't even *try* for a single, solitary date, well … He has to shake his own head in disbelief. How can it be that when he *stopped* looking, love crashed straight into his life?

"All of this, Greg," Lindsey continues. "Each pin in my map, each stop, each town along the way …" She motions to the marker line wavering to the map's lone remaining pushpin. "It all led me *here*—all of it—to Addison." When she pauses once more, Greg raises his hands to her face and bends even closer to hear her soft voice. "It all led me here, to you."

When he glances away, not truly believing her words, snow is falling again outside the window. The flakes spin and lazily twirl from the sky. Greg looks back at Lindsey to be certain she meant it. Again, she nods. And she tips her head, watching him.

Waiting.

So he touches her cheek, and steps even closer in her tiny house that somehow has all the room he needs. He slips his hand behind her neck, bends and kisses her. Once. Then again, longer.

Outside, the winter wind blows, and those crystal snowflakes whisper against the windowpane. Lindsey leans into him and deepens their kiss so that he can't help it, the way he cradles her face and holds her as though he can never let go. Kisses her that way, too—until he stops and touches her cheek, her neck. But only for a second, because he can't be away from their kiss that long. So then, he kisses her once more, softly, while fighting back his own tears. Tears at the realization of how love blew into his life like one of winter's first flurries—surprising and enchanting and seemingly out of nowhere.

"Greg," Lindsey whispers, dropping her hands to around his waist while smiling into the kiss that neither wants to end. "Merry Christmas," she tells him, this time pulling slightly back and touching his whiskered jaw.

The cold wind still whistles outside the tiny house, and fresh snow dusts the window edges. Behind the sudden flurry, the lights of the lakeside Christmas tree blur—streaked by the swirling snow squall.

Greg sees it all for merely a moment.

But it feels like one moment too many to be looking away from Lindsey as her fingers touch his hair, his face. So he takes her hand in his, holds it to his heart and watches only her when he says, "Merry Christmas, Lindsey Haynes."

ENJOY MORE OF
THE WINTER NOVELS

1) Snowflakes and Coffee Cakes

2) Snow Deer and Cocoa Cheer

3) Cardinal Cabin

4) First Flurries

5) Eighteen Winters

FROM NEW YORK TIMES BESTSELLING AUTHOR

JOANNE DEMAIO

Also by Joanne DeMaio

The Winter Novels
(In Order)
1) Snowflakes and Coffee Cakes
2) Snow Deer and Cocoa Cheer
3) Cardinal Cabin
4) First Flurries
5) Eighteen Winters
—And More Winter Novels—

The Seaside Saga
(In order)
1) Blue Jeans and Coffee Beans
2) The Denim Blue Sea
3) Beach Blues
4) Beach Breeze
5) The Beach Inn
6) Beach Bliss
7) Castaway Cottage
8) Night Beach
9) Little Beach Bungalow
10) Every Summer
11) Salt Air Secrets
12) Stony Point Summer
13) The Beachgoers
—And More Seaside Saga Books—

Summer Standalone Novels
True Blend
Whole Latte Life

Novella
The Beach Cottage

For a complete list of books by New York Times
bestselling author Joanne DeMaio, visit:

Joannedemaio.com

About the Author

JOANNE DEMAIO is a *New York Times* and *USA Today* bestselling author of contemporary fiction. She enjoys writing about friendship, family, love and choices, while setting her stories in New England towns or by the sea. Joanne lives with her family in Connecticut and is currently at work on her next novel.

For a complete list of books and for news on upcoming releases, please visit Joanne's website. She also enjoys hearing from readers on Facebook.

Author Website:
www.joannedemaio.com

Facebook:
www.facebook.com/JoanneDeMaioAuthor